ESCAPE

Katlin Murray

Copyright © 2014 Katlin Murray
All rights reserved.
ISBN: 1530967864
ISBN-13: 978-1530967865

For my Dad

ACKNOWLEDGMENTS

Many thanks to my family for their devoted support, to my parents for encouraging me to imagine and to my husband, Alan, for his patience and artistic inspiration; without you all this book would be quietly collecting dust on my shelves, you gave me the courage to share my stories with the world, I am eternally grateful.

PROLOGUE

It all started with a letter, tucked away neatly where only the right person would find it:

"You always played the Princess, now it is your turn to play the prince. A damsel in distress waits in a tower for a knight in shining armour."

It read in a delicate scrawl, sealed in a small frail envelope that looked as though it would crumble to dust at the slightest touch. Luckily it hadn't, for the series of events that were to follow rang similar in severity to the fabled tales heard in childhood. Sadly when momentous events like these occur in the real world they are less filled with flowers and fauna and more engulfed in smoke and fire. The delicacy of human nature is a raw thing, often overlooked in the span of a story. Sometimes, however, it is the things that we overlook that are the most important in the end.

TOWER

Ten years had passed since the fatal day on the school yard that had changed her future forever. She was sure she had once had hopes of being a mediocre student, going to a mediocre college and perhaps even getting a job she liked. Maybe she had hoped to move out of town on her own, but really she hadn't thought that far ahead and her chance to dream had been cut short with her kidnapping.

Instead, she was locked in the bell tower of an abandoned church. The walls of her cell were rough and worn from her pacing and their former abandon.

Grace had been moved every couple of years until settling down in the tower, usually whenever she tried to escape. For some reason that place had stuck. She was approaching the five year mark. It had become a familiar place to her. For the first two years in the tower the windows had been boarded over and it had been gloomy. Grace had lived in a constant darkness, relying on her other senses and the thin lines of light that escaped through the boarded windows to get through the daily routines she kept.

She had tried to pry the boards loose after two years of darkness and had been caught as the first draft of fresh air washed through the window.

They had locked her in a cage in the cellar for a week and replaced the

ESCAPE

boards with one way coated glass, unbreakable. Only then had she finally had a view of the world again. After that she could see the sky. Light would filter through the windows during the day and at night the stars and distant city lights were usually enough to give her sight. At first the wonder had hurt her eyes.

Then she became familiar with the stars in the sky. She could sit there for hours counting the stars or making shapes out of the clouds. It was only the frivolousness of wasting her time that stopped her from sitting at the window staring at the sky all day every day. She longed to one day be out on the other side of the glass looking up. That kept her motivated enough to stay away from the looking glass.

She paced her small tower room day in and day out, watching the outside world enviously as she worked. Her hopes of being rescued were long gone after endless sunsets had come and gone on the other side of the mirrored windows that the world saw from outside her tower. She had long since relied only on herself. Even the guards that watched her tower door were not dependable for providing her with food on a regular basis. She had come to discover that *"Nine am"* was just an expression the guards used when they remembered that she hadn't been fed yet. Still, to her it remained an alarm of sorts. Letting her know when she was being monitored and when they were just there absorbed in their own lives.

She spent most nights working through her own escape plans while enduring a series of trials she had developed to help build her strength and stamina up. She knew that with her minimal diet and the living condition she was trapped in, she needed to work twice as hard to obtain the endurance that would be necessary to enact her own escape. She would recite the guards' shifts for the week under her breath while sprinting on the spot, keeping her pace fast and steady until she could breathe through the week schedule without panting or breaking a sweat. She would practice tying knots with sheets and escaping from them in less than ten seconds, just in case she was tied and dragged between dungeons again in the future.

She had every intention of fighting back for her freedom. She would often find herself lost in thoughts of her old life aimlessly doing crunches or push-ups tirelessly while the moon swept across the towers floor in the dead of night. On the little food she was provided with she remained quite scrawny in appearance, though most of her mass was wiry muscle.

When the guards would switch for the evening she would begin, choosing to spend most daylight hours doing more productive escape preparations that required the light to see. At dawn Grace would take a moment to admire the sun hanging low on the horizon and then toss her tired body at the lumpy mattress on her old tattered bed frame and sleep soundly until the nine a.m. alarm of the guards shoving food through the door. With their accuracy, some days she got more sleep than others. She could tell if they were on time or daftly late by the shadows across her walls.

The routine worked quite well for her and kept her on her toes as she gave herself a purpose behind the tower walls. She looked forward to a life with more meaning, a life beyond the gates and the enslavement of the church.

The church that held her above the land of the living, in its decrepit bell tower, had stood abandoned to the outside world for decades. It had crumbled under years of abandonment and neglect, much like the life that it held fast in its embrace.

No one bothered to take note of the flurry of activity that took place twice a day as the guards would change shifts, scurrying out to their cars as the newcomers dawdled on their way in. Cars would whip from the parking lot like they were destined for the Grand Prix as they shot through the gates and back into the world.

Construction signs sat unused inside the church gates, proof that the town had forgotten the monumental landmark that had once glistened on the hill above them. It had provided them a refuge and home in times of need. The neglected church had been replaced like so many other things by a newer, bigger and better model, full of technology; leaving the heritage and history in the dust as people moved on.

Asides from the sparkling new windows in the bell tower where Grace resided, the rest of the building had fallen into a dangerous state of disrepair. Trees leaned on the tall stone wall surrounding the property, leaving boulders teetering on the edge of the precipice waiting to fall wayward as the trees decayed and more weight pressed against the crumbling mortar of the old walls. Some boulders had already fallen, rolling across the lawn and at the church walls like bowling balls trying to take out the building.

She had watched as stones rolled against the main building sending cracks spreading across the already worn foundation. Holes were visible in the main building roof and presumably in the tower, which leaked heavily whenever it rained.

It would drip in a stream onto her bed making the floors slippery for days at a time. She would curl up in the corner farthest from the door where the floor seemed to be raised up on a strange angle and wait out the water, shivering when the air became stagnant and mouldy.

Grace had grown accustomed to the crumbling building, passing her more tedious hours counting the cracks and missing stone on the exterior that was visible from her vantage. On particularly windy days she would watch as the shingles slid off into the sky. Some days she half expected that the building itself would decay and crumble away with her inside, blowing away into the adjacent trees and disappearing forever in the wind. At this point she only hoped she would make it out alive when the building gave up on her.

Grace would watch the sun set over the town and the sun rise over the forest. The glow always gave her hope as she fought through her mediocre days.

She watched the guards leave and come for their shifts, noting which way they turned at the end of the drive each day as though it were an indication of whether or not they were coming back. She made up stories about their social lives outside the church based on the direction they took at the end of their shift. When they turned to the forest she imagined them driving a winding scenic route taking them to their immaculate homes and happy families. When they turned to the town she would imagine them in a tavern letting loose with their buddies, leaving the details of their secret job to the fates as they pretended to be spies and heroes rather than kidnappers and dungeon guards.

Grace felt like a spy sometimes, watching the outside world change as buildings popped up on the horizon, all from her secret room. She remembered every detail as though it were life threatening. She could never be sure what information could help lead to her escape. She imagined herself as a pedestrian walking by the church sometimes, wondering what it looked like to the outside world. Did they see it as she did, like a decaying prison? Or was it something more; a monument, a castle or something spectacular? Would anyone ever notice that she was up there?

She had been plotting since the moment she had been thrown into the small room, mercilessly colliding with the splintered wooden floorboards as her bound hands were unable to break her fall. The door had slammed and locked behind her as she struggled to get free of her bindings through the chloroform haze that had kept her under for the transfer in the form of a pillowcase tied over her head.

She had been caught trying to escape from the basement of another property, where they had held her before the dark days of the tower. They had drugged her and moved her like any other transfer. She had been treated like a bag of potatoes, tossed from car to car, bag over her face, drenched in toxic chemicals to keep her hazy. She would never know where she had come from and until the windows had been installed in the tower, she had never known to where she had been taken.

In her mind the tower had been another underground prison, all the same musty mouldy smells had mingled in the walls and floors. The dampness had been the same, the leaking and the darkness fooling her and coercing impossible escape plans. Until the day she had discovered how high up she really was.

She analysed her failed attempts over and over again in the dark of night. Pinpointing the things that had gotten her caught the why's and the how's, trying to ensure that her next escape stuck. The first two years she had tried to visualize the room based on feel. The darkness seemed a punishment for trying to run away. When the windows had been put in place things had become easier for her, the height had been her biggest obstacle to overcome. How would she get down from the tower unscathed and *able* to get help?

Patience, she hoped, would ensure that her fifth escape attempt would be a success.

She stood by one of the windows, watching the city as she tirelessly chipped away at the seal inside the trim. It was autumn, another year locked away, alone. Her red hair had matted into a tangled sheet down her back. She hadn't seen her own face since she was ten, save for dusty reflections in pools of water that often collected on the floor in the spring. At nearly twenty one, she was unaware of her delicate beauty and the way she looked like a princess even under the grime and tangles.

Her clothing was simple, drawstring pants and a shirt, baggy and oversized. At least over the years she had somewhat grown in to them. She could tell they were not new and rarely washed properly. The fabric was worn thin at the knees, ready to rip at the slightest touch.

Every two weeks she was asked to place her hands out the hole in the door where her meals came through to be hand cuffed. She would then turn to the wall and the guards would come in and replace her linens and toiletries, only the bare minimum. She suspected it was an order to be rude to her. They usually didn't even bother acknowledging her existence, save for the days when they had to come in. When they had completed their inspection, they would lock the door and un-cuff her hands through the door when they were ready. They would often leave her sitting with her arms dangling out the door slot for hours on end waiting.

Grace was cautious to hide the chips from the window trim, along with anything else that may be suspicious and draw unwanted attention. She needed to be there long enough to escape. She needed them not to move her again. But the guards had grown lazy over the years and she could hear by the shuffles of their feet and the squeaking of the floorboards that they now only tossed in the new sheets, clothing, and soap, without searching. They let the items scatter across the floor like an explosion of supplies.

Sometimes she spent more time finding pieces of soap than she did using it. A toilet and sink sat against the wall closest the door and that was where Grace washed herself, using her fingers to comb through her unruly hair. She was rarely given a chance to speak, unless it was to herself. The guards wouldn't answer when she called. She preferred it that way. It gave her more time to think. The odd conversation she would hear outside the door in her silence proved to be entertainment enough for someone so accustomed to silence.

Grace fondly remembered a time when she had hot water, bubble baths and showers. She missed the little things more; noise, laughter maybe even ice cream. In the tower her meals were simple; rice, protein shakes and water from her tap. The shakes wouldn't be so bad, if the guards didn't drink them half up before giving them to her when they forgot their own lunches. She had never thought as a child she would one day wish for vegetables. Even broccoli would be a welcome addition to the slop she ate daily. The texture alone was enough to put her off of eating. It was always room temperature and stale. It was like the years supply sat pre-made on a shelf outside the door, just waiting to be served to her and each day it got worse as it grew closer to its expiration.

"This is the year." Grace muttered, as she chipped away another piece of trim. She hoped the guard wouldn't hear the noise she was making. "They never come in here anyway…" She whispered in a quiet sing song voice.

Still, she wished she could be quieter and held her breath hoping to compensate by not breathing loudly for a moment. She watched the town as she worked. It looked small and fake, like the buildings were meant for little dolls and fancy wooden furniture you could hold in your hand. It reminded her of a dollhouse she had once had and as the light hit each of the gleaming windows of the village at the bottom of the hill she couldn't escape the feeling that she was in a fairytale; locked in a castle tower, awaiting a prince.

It was a feeling that had left her bitter inside. The children's' stories she had loved in her youth had mislead her. They always depicted the rescued princesses as being happy or content with what they had, even before their prince arrived. Grace struggled with the concept that they had really been as miserable as she was, trapped in their own nightmares. They were probably tired of waiting when their princes *did* arrive. Grace wasn't going to wait. She would not leave her freedom up to chance or in someone else's hands.

She would just have to save herself or die trying.

The property surrounding the church was large with thick, tall stone walls hiding it from the outside world. It sat like a fortress in solitude, separated from the town by the steep incline of the hill it decorated. The forest grew around it, ever nearer as it encroached on to the property inch by inch, year after year.

The fiery trees dotting the edges of the forest had already lost most of their leaves onto the church grounds. Grace had watched them as their greens melded into yellows, oranges and reds.

From her tower Grace could see beyond the walls and into the village streets. Fancy stores dotted the main street just a few blocks away, closest to the winding road that lead to the church drive.

Most people from the town did not venture out her way. Occasionally a stray teenager or two would get close to the property, snooping around the grounds like they were approaching a haunted house. Then the ground security guard would confront them, usually putting on a show of calling for backup that would send the kids scrambling for the trees.

They were never caught. The guards were far too lazy to chase anyone anyway. Grace was sure there was some sort of scary legend keeping most of the kids away and only the bravest ones wandering out from the trees on Halloween night, trying to get a sneak peek of the creepy church in the moonlight. They usually took off quickly, afraid of getting police involved or their parents called. The truth was the guards were not allowed to call the police; they would risk Grace being found.

Sometimes while she was watching a group of teens dash wildly back into the woods at night, she wondered how that conversations would go if the police ever *did* show up at the church. Even if they moved her out in secret, how do you explain the living arrangements set up in the bell tower of an abandoned church that was being renovated?

Grace had been chipping away at the window trim for months. She

ESCAPE

was getting close enough to test out her escape plan. This time she had prepared for everything, tucking away helpful things for a couple of years now. She was ready to leave the tower. And after years of tracking, she even knew where the closest police station was.

She had watched their cars and plotted their routes, knowing it could make or break her escape. She would need their help once she was free of the tower if she hoped to remain a part of the outside world and avoid being sucked back into oblivion.

It was almost the day. She was growing nervous anticipating the adrenaline rush of freedom, pouring over every detail in calculated concentration. The morning guards were always a little sluggish and the night guards were quick to make their own escape as their duty ended. No one stopped to chat at morning shift change and Grace could sneak away before they had a chance to finish their coffees and forget to feed her.

It would be perfect.

KNIGHT

As he trudged through the forest towards the church, he felt a looming dread. He had assured them that the plan was fail safe. It was better that they be kept in the dark until it was time. Too much noise was sure to wake the sleeping dragon, a cost he could not afford just yet.

The leaves crunched ominously under his feet, threatening to give him away. Soon night would be falling and he was ready. Crouched in the woods he went over the plan in his head for a final time as the sun sunk lower in the sky. He waited for the right moment, hoping his timing was as impeccable as it was in his head.

Steeling himself for the scourge, he pulled a grappling hook from his shoulder. Unraveling the trail of rope onto the ground beside him, he approached the wall. He sized it up, taking one last breath as he paced looking to the tower, his goal. With a grand swing he launched his arm into the air letting the hook rise in an arc. The hook passed the wall colliding with the other side of the stone. Tugging back to test the hook, it was unsecure and toppled back towards his feet landing with a loud thud inches from his toes.

He flinched. Bracing himself, he tried again, cautiously lopping the hook over the chipped stone facade. Rocks tumbled to his feet loudly over the silent evening, but the hook remained secure giving him a chance to clamour over.

Pulling himself up, he felt elation looming closer than ever. The tower shone in the setting sun, a beacon of hope. Mirrors reflecting the sky gave the tower a strange look, like it held the sunset trapped inside its stone arches, a prisoner in the dark of night. The windows shone like diamonds against the decaying rocks and collapsing roof that held above.

He took an extra moment at the top of the rock wall, looking at the strange sight in awe of its rustic beauty. When he landed he scrambled for cover knowing the guards were the next obstacle on his quest to the inner tower walls.

He felt like a knight, armoured and on the rescue mission of his life. He was ready to prove his worthiness and although the adrenaline rush was powering him through. The closer he got to the tower, the more he fought to get inside. He felt as though his very life depended upon getting up into the bell tower of the decrepit church before it crumbled at his feet from decay.

One of the guards was close. He could hear footsteps in the yard, maybe the rustling of leaves if he really strained his ears. He dashed from tree to bush for cover, making his way to the open church doors with cautious calculations. He tumbled into a bush, taking a face full of dirt to avoid making too much sound. As he stopped to catch his bearings, he looked over the grounds from the cover of the brambles around him.

The church doors appeared before him, vacant and ajar. Propped open for fresh air and to carry out the moulding stench that wafted from within its walls. He searched the area between himself and the door with cautious shifting eyes, wary that he hadn't seen a guard yet and with one last leap he raced to the opening sprinting as fast as his legs would carry.

He hit the front steps and felt a tug on his shoulder. Before he could catch himself, he fell to the ground. *Shit*, he thought as he slammed into the worn edges of the steps.

He had hoped to avoid the guards for a while longer. It was going to make it more difficult to get in now. The messenger bag on his shoulder spilled its contents across the steps as it ripped down the seam. It fell from his side as he struggled, scattering coils of rope and files across the stoop. They tumbled into the muddy grass as they rolled away no longer of any use to him in his mission.

The plan had changed and it was time to roll with the punches.

Rolling over, he kicked out fiercely with a wild well of rage and hit the guard in the hand.

A gun fired .

A look of shock registered across the guards face, freezing him for a moment as he wondered where his bullet had escaped to. When he had caught himself, the guard leapt forward and pinned his intruder with knees to the arms. Sitting heavily on his chest, the guard reached for a radio.

"Walt, I need backup." He growled, gasping at the exertion. It was soon followed by a muffled ,"On my way."

It was not going as planned.

The guard kicked him over using a reserve of energy that had likely been uncalled on for some years. He gasped as he pulled the tie from his uniform while sitting heavily on top to bind the struggling man's hands behind his back. The knot was useless, but it was enough to keep his hands in one place while the guard dragged him through the door into the church.

As he was dragged into the church an overwhelming dread passed through him. He had just awoken the dragon. His muscles seized up as he bucked against the callous tugs of the guard at his feet. He scraped against the rough splintery floor, fighting to get back into the evening air. If he was discovered and brought before the beast, they would all be killed and until now the gravity of the situation had failed to sink in.

The floor was rough and splintered at his face while the man pulled at his feet. Once through the blistered archway, his feet were dropped with a loud clunk against the wooden floorboards, sending a plume of dirt and sawdust up into his eyes. He blinked rapidly trying to clear his vision as a door across the room opened and a second guard entered.

The floor was infested with termites. Looking across to the door he could see sections of the floor that were ready to collapse into the ground, worn through with footsteps and failed renovations. He could see the lines where the pews had once stood. Now all that was left was a vacant room of staring angels, broken in their teetering pewter glass frames. They had been boarded in patches to keep the outside world away. It was horrifying to look at the once beautiful masterpiece of the old town, now fallen to ruin at the hands of the devil himself.

"Take him to the cellar." The new guard demanded, standing framed in a doorway. Light spilled out behind him, his voice was deep and he towered over the first guard as he walked into the room seemingly in charge.

"Give me a hand Walt." whined the man at his feet, looking like a powerless child struggling with a backpack after school.

Walt took a foot, rolling his eyes to the ceiling in disgust. They dragged him to the door on the other side of the room where Walt had first entered. He squirmed, fighting back. He tried to get his arms loose to fight, fearing that if he was dragged any farther into the madness of that place he would be set to face Lucifer, the dragon of the castle.

One of his feet hit the floor again. He looked up into the eyes of the scruffy large guard holding his gun out of the holster at his waist, pointed just slightly, enough to aim at his heart.

"Don't make me give you a reason to fight." His voice echoed in the almost empty room, the glass angels looked on in silence from their wilted thrones.

"I'll mess you up kid." He grunted into the stale air taking a short intimidating lunge at his prey before returning to his feet.

A moment later the dragging resumed and he was tugged over the threshold of the small door. He looked back into the vacant room one last time as the angels were pulled out of sight.

On the other side, a set of worn stone steps hammered at his cheek, he fought the urge to fight back. He knew that the gun was still in Walt's hand, ready to take a piece off of him if he gave a reason. His arms, still bound behind his back, offered little resistance to his battered face.

The air was mouldy and tickled at his nose as he struggled to breath between the hammering of the steps against his body. He resisted the urge to sneeze, fearing the impending pain of the hard steps. His shoulder had taken much of the jarring force of each stone edge, yet his face throbbed in protest. The staircase grew steeper as the light of the upper floor faded slowly away.

The stone of the steps gave way to dirt and gravel as the staircase came to an abrupt end. Sections of the floor seemed harder, as if the underlay was wood planks, lost under years of debris. The room was dark and cluttered with the gutted remains of the now empty main floor of the church. Large splinters from broken pews clung at his clothing as he was dragged a few feet into the space. The guards fumbled trying to retain their grasp as they reached for their flashlights, no longer able to see in the dim fading light filtering from the stairwell.

"Tie him to a post, I'll check on the girl." Said the smaller of the two, suddenly acting like the boss.

The guard turned against the dark short room and sprinted up the stairs slowly, leaving him fending against the tall hulking beast called Walt.

He could hear the footsteps of the smaller guard stumbling up the stairs as he raced away from his duties.

When the first guard was out of sight Walt spoke again, "I'm not paid enough for this crap." He snipped staring into his victims eyes for a moment too long.

Lifting his flashlight over his head, he swung it down, cracking it over the intruders head with a deafening thud of metal hitting skull.

He held on for a moment longer as blood began to trickle down his forehead and into his eye, in a haze he could see the flashlight being lifted again, he blinked against the glare of the bulb.

Then the world went dark.

ESCAPE

As dusk approached, Grace stared out the window watching the dark slithering over the scarcely full trees of the forest. The bare branches reached into the dark oblivion of the sky giving her the chills. Soon they would all be barren and it would be another year locked up for her. She looked at the stone wall and a movement caught her eye.

A shadowy figure was moving along the stone wall, coming from the woods on the other side.

It could be an animal, Grace thought leaning in to the glass for a better look. A person wouldn't be in the woods that late, not even a hunter. Grace watched as the figure paced the wall, throwing something over the edge. Her curiosity peaked , she stood, pressing her hands to the glass in wonder.

The shape disappeared for a moment lost in the shadow of the stone wall and she found herself standing on her tip toes to look for whatever it was. She watched as a rope swung above the wall, disappearing back into the forest. A moment later it reappeared, crossing over the wall and hooking to a rock at the top.

Grace stared on, puzzled by the development. Then the dark shape came looming over the top of the wall pausing at the top like a large jungle cat before dropping heavily in the church yard below. It scampered off into a bush before she could get a good look.

Someone had climbed the wall. Her brain was screaming at her while her curiosity turned into horror; *someone has climbed the wall!*

The shape neared the church, sneaking through the trees as if hiding from a predator. Only Grace from her vantage point could see the movement of the shadowy shape as it lunged from tree to tree like a wisp of smoke, tucking into the branches and disappearing for moments at a time before swirling back out unexpectedly, leaping closer to the door.

The ground level guard exited the church doors to go for his perimeter check. Grace held her breath as the shape leapt from within a bush to reach the door. The guard yelped and a gunshot fired into the silence sending Grace jumping back across her small room in shock. She stared at the wall in a daze for a moment wondering how it would affect her predicament.

Grace heard a shuffle outside her door. She skittered quietly over, pressing her ear against the soft wood to listen. She heard a muffled static and then the guard on the intercom.

"On my way." He shouted, sounding panicked. His chair scraped across the floor falling over with a clatter. Grace scrambled to clean up her mess, scraping the pile of dust and broken trim under her bed and stashing the fork she had kept under her mattress. She quietly sat, picking up the book Walter the guard had let her have three years ago, waiting to see where his hurried footsteps would take him.

Romeo and Juliet, she still had never read it, yet it was worn from all the times she had pretended.

The chair in the hall scraped against the floor as it was pulled upright. Walter was leaving. Footsteps, loud and heavy down the rickety stairs that led to her door told her something was wrong. The intruder had caused them to set off the alarms.

Doors were slamming.

The guards were shouting to one another in the distance below her. Grace stood to see out the window. Someone was trying to fight his way in.

Who would want so badly to break IN to an emancipated building like this? Grace thought. And what would they think when they realised there were guards stationed there? Maybe it would make the news. Maybe someone would investigate and maybe they would find her!

Or, thought Grace bitterly, maybe they would kill him and maybe they would move her. Then she would have to start her escape all over again.

She was about to lose five years worth of plotting and planning. All of her hard work thrown out the window because a stranger decided to have a look at the creepy church at the top of the hill.

Grace sat quietly by the window watching as the guard kicked the man, tied his arms and dragged him back through the front doors. She was sure as he was turned towards the building he had looked right at her, but she knew the glass was mirrored on his side.

He didn't know she was up there. Still she scowled back at the face that had ruined her almost perfect escape.

Two minutes passed and the commotion downstairs had quieted down. Her heart was beating heavily in her chest as she contemplated her options. She still hadn't heard Walter return up the stairs with his heavy shoes on the wooden steps;

"This is it." Whispered Grace, turning to her bed shakily.

She had been waiting for a distraction for months, hoping for the right moment to test her escape plan before she had settled for the morning espionage she had planned for the next day. Her schedule would be moving up just slightly and she hoped that her nerves would quickly be calmed by the rush of adrenaline that was pouring through her veins at the thought of freedom.

Grace darted under her mattress retrieving the fork and a small pillowcase of things she had gathered over the years that she thought might be helpful when it came down to the wire. Hairpins, extra clothing that she had tucked away before they had become too worn through, and some granola bars that she had saved from meals when Walter had enjoyed her protein shake and given her something from his own lunch to replace it.

It was enough to get by, she hoped, if she had to take cover for a while to get to the police station safely. She didn't expect it to take her long to reach the police station in the close by town of Monticello. She had grown up there before the kidnapping and vaguely remembered the streets by sight, never having seen them from the birds' eye vantage until three years ago.

It had twisted her perspective of the town slightly. She knew how long it should take her to get over the wall and down the sloped hill into town, having timed it in her head nearly every night, pace for pace. She looked out the window one last time before darting across the room for her things. She moved back to the window excitedly, using the fork to pry the glass in; just enough that she could grab it by hand. She ducked down as she pulled it back.

"This should work." She grunted as her arms strained, pulling against the resistance of the remaining trim. With a strange sucking sound the glass came free, she smiled with wide eyes. It was heavier than she expected. She teetered, holding the panel with two cautious hands hoping not to slice them open before it fell at her feet in a large piece. Only one crack appeared, running up the middle of the previously shatterproof guard.

Stepping back before it fell on her, she quickly reached under her bed for the pile of linens she had hoarded over the last few years. All tied perfectly with the knots she had practiced, and strong enough to support her weight all the way to the ground. She fastened the end to the post of the bed, like she had seen in movies as a child. Pulling the glass across the room and out of her way she carefully pushed the remainder of the linen out through the open window. She tugged her bed closer to the gaping hole, knowing it would move anyway when she started down the wall.

She froze as the stairs began to creak. It was Steve, the other security guard. She could tell by the lighter footfalls and the hesitation at the top. She hadn't expected they would be done with the intruder so soon. She hadn't heard any more gunfire and no one else had arrived at the grounds to take him away. Moving as quietly as she could, Grace messed up her sheets enough to cover up the obvious escape attempt and turned to sit on her mattress. She hid her pillowcase behind her as she stared at the closed door separating her from Steve. She hoped he wouldn't come in. She needed more time to cover this up so she could try again in the morning.

That is if she was still there when the sun rose. Grace was flustered. The intruder had ruined her escape with his horrible timing.

There came a knock on the door followed shortly by a brisk, "I'm coming in." Steve jangled his keys to unlock her door.

Grace panicked. She knew they would move her if they saw the window off and her sheet rope dangling out, to another tower, to another room. Five years wasted plotting her escape. All ruined by one mysterious stranger. It wasn't fair. Grace would not give up without a fight. As the doorknob turned, she made up her mind. Sneaking behind the door she waited.

Steve stepped into the room timidly, as though she were the criminal in this situation and not he, "Grace, Grace where are you?" He demanded in a sing song voice.

As he was taking a step further in past the door Grace stepped out into sight. She swung her pillowcase filled with the supplies she had saved at the side of his head, causing him to drop his keys as he stumbled reaching to protect his face. He tripped over the sheet of glass into the side of her lumpy bed. Grace scooped the keys up and raced out the door defiantly slamming it as she fumbled for the correct key to lock it back up with Steve inside.

She could hear him swearing at her from the other side as she dropped the keys to the floor. He pounded against the door, barely moving it against its frame. Grace stopped a second to take in her new surroundings. She had only seen that side of the door once.

It had been three years ago when the old guard Derrick had accidentally left the door unlocked after delivering her supplies. She had snuck out then with her arms still shackled, only to be caught moments later fleeing down the stairs. It would be different this time; Grace knew she had to be careful. Being captured this time would mean starting her escape plans all over somewhere new and that was if they let her live through another transfer.

With one guard locked up and the other preoccupied, she hoped she had enough time to get free. She knew Steve would radio Walter to tell him what had happened, backup would be called. But in that moment she was running for her freedom.

Grace crept down the stairs careful to avoid any creaking in the wooden steps as she kept her pace fast and light. The tower stairs wound round and down for what seemed like forever. She crept, as stealthily as she could, knowing how much noise the guards usually made when they were barging up and down in their heavy boots. She didn't want to tip Walt off wherever he was in the church.

Grace had never been that far down the stairs. She wished they would end soon. A door appeared in the wall at a short landing, but the stairs continued on. Grace stopped to check the knob but the door was locked; she would have to continue on.

Several spirals later Grace found herself at an opening as the end of the stairs collided with a rough stone arch leading into a dank dark space that smelled wet and earthy. Grace was thrilled, she had missed the smells of the outside world and the dark was nothing new for her. The tower had had no lights, only windows to let in the sun. As Grace crept into the blackened room, she heard a shuffle above her.

The floorboards above her head creaked and she listened to Walter speaking. "Sir, its Grace, she has left her tower… yes sir, we have him…No Sir… yes Sir… right away Sir… We'll be expecting them…Thank you, Sir."

The footsteps moved away and Grace heard footfalls ascending the stairs. Walter was on his way to retrieve Steve. It sounded like they had called for reinforcements at last. Luckily reinforcements were rarely given the whole story and would take a while to get to the remote church.

It would risk too many people knowing about Grace's predicament. Judging from her previous experiences that meant she was relatively safe, for a while at least.

CELLAR

Taking a moment to let her eyes adjust to the dim room, Grace calculated that she had overshot the main floor. She had luckily missed a run in with Walt, thanks to a locked door. Somehow she had made it to the unused basement of the church.

A familiar cage sat in a far corner. It was where she had lived like an animal for the weeks while her windows were installed. Smiling at it she now realized that her own screams had probably instigated the ghost stories that had kept the town folk far away.

A faint glow emitted down the stairwell from the light at the landing above. In the faint glimmer Grace could see the shape of the room extending before her. The ceiling hung low, showing the exposed beams and floorboards of the main floor drooping in places as the floor above slowly eroded away and would soon collapse into the disorder around her.

Piles of broken church pews and podiums consumed the space. She quietly made her way through the room avoiding the rickety rubbish that had been stacked randomly throughout the space. She was cautious of her bare feet as she stepped forward, searching for a window, door, anything that might aid her in her escape to the outside world. She knew it would be unsafe for her to try the main floor. Even if the door was unlocked that was where they would be waiting for her.

No, she thought, if she couldn't get out then she would hide and hope they didn't burn the church to the ground looking for her.

Grace stifled her breath as the guards paced overhead. When they returned to the main floor one set of footprints raced out the front door. They were probably searching the property in case she had exited while they were on the stairs.

It was then that she realised someone else was in the room with her, breathing heavily from across a pile of rubbish. She froze catching her breath as she looked back into the room and away from the floorboards above.

Grace crept nearer to the source of the sound making sure to keep mounds of debris between her and the heavy breathing in case it was a guard she didn't know about. Grace knew there was always one outside her door and another on the main floor. She had no idea whether or not the basement was guarded. It had been while she was locked down in the cage and she kicked herself at the thought that she had forgotten. She took extra precaution with her steps, afraid that she had overlooked a significant detail, one that could ruin her escape.

As Grace peeked around a rotted out pew, a voice startled her.

"You don't need to be so quiet, I know you're here." It rasped, growing bolder. "Did you come back to beat me again, because I won't tell you anything." The voice paused to cough as Grace crept closer, stepping softly across the room, "Or have they told you to kill me yet, lock me up like they did the girl." Grace stopped in wonder. He continued; "Hide me away from the world?" After a brief pause the voice became impatient "Well! Show yourself you useless criminal, stop wasting my time!"

"Shh..." Grace whispered. She found herself and stepped from behind the pew. *That must be the man from the yard*, she thought as she stopped short.

She was wary of getting too close. She was concerned, he had known about the tower prison. *Who is he?* She wondered as she peered forward, willing her eyes to adjust enough to make out his features. He appeared as a dark shadow before her. He was still, save for the movement of his laboured breathing. He sounded as though he had asthma and the damp mould of the cellar was clearly a trigger.

Her eyes slowly focused and she began to make out more detail in the shape that loomed before her. The man appeared to be slightly older than Grace. He was tall with short dark hair. He stooped under the low ceiling of the cellar. He didn't look to be very muscular, his slim awkward build seemed to explain how the guards took him in so easily.

Why had he come barging in so gallantly, throwing himself into danger? He couldn't have expected to get past the guards. His mouth dropped in shock when he saw her and it appeared that he knew more about her situation than even the guards knew.

"Who are you?" Grace asked in a demanding whisper. She quickly realised that this was the first person she had talked to in ten years, unless you counted talking to yourself.

The man stared at Grace for a moment too long. A strange look passed across his face with what Grace was sure was a quick smile. The moment passed awkwardly as she stared back, he returned to a somber stare looking to the ground embarrassed.

"Perhaps it would be best to talk in detail later…" He started mumbling at his feet, "My name is Ethan." He looked up expectantly as she stared back at him with astonishment.

"I came here to get you out." The embarrassment was back on his face again as he shrugged awkwardly.

Grace stepped forward timidly checking him over. Could it really be? "Ethan? As in Ethan Evans?" She cautiously queried, looking him over with more attention to detail.

The narrow features of his face were similar to that of the boy she once knew by that name. She furrowed her brow, concentrating on what she could remember of her old friends' features.

"One in the same." Ethan put forth, hanging his head in shame, "I'm so sorry it took me this long….Grace…" He trailed off for a second, "…someone left me a note…it took me a while to figure it out…" He continued trailing off into a mumble, almost to himself.
Grace's smile beamed across to Ethan. He looked up, caught in her beauty and couldn't help but smile back. She timidly reached out to touch his face in disbelief. She had been alone for so long and a day before she tried to escape, there he was, tied in the basement after jumping the wall.

She couldn't help but laugh, he always was a fool. Quickly catching herself she looked up to the beam above her head. Covering her mouth, she paused for a moment listening and hoping she hadn't just tipped the guards off.

Grace and Ethan had been childhood companions, their fathers had worked together. And at times, Ethan's family had been more like a family than she could ever remember her father being. She had spent countless summer days and even school nights at the Evans' estate. The Evans' family butler had cared for Grace and Ethan while their fathers did business, usually out of town. She had missed him and felt a tremendous amount of guilt as she looked into his dark brown eyes.

She had watched his father die.

Ethan stood, bound to a post that likely supported the loose floorboards above. He was tied at the hands with what appeared to be a cheap necktie. She quickly weighed her options; trying to pass the guards on her own, not even knowing what was beyond the walls of the church, or taking Ethan with her for the small amount of help he may provide. It wasn't a difficult choice considering the suicide mission he had embarked on to get there.

Grace approached Ethan cautiously, eyes lingering on his face, now rough with age. He was no longer the young boy she once confided in. He appeared worn, likely from the very events that had led to her predicament as well. Grace felt sympathy for Ethan. She wished she could tell him what had happened to his father but it was not the time, not while their safety hung in peril. She tenderly reached out to the binding neck-tie, smirking as she discovered that it was wound so simply around his wrists that he could have undone it himself, if he had only tried.

"What was the plan?" Grace inquired timidly as she checked Ethan over for cuts and bruises. Peering intently across the storage room, she waited for his reply.

"First we get you out…" responded Ethan. He was quick to jump into action once his arms were free. Stretching them out, he winced at the numbness. "…then we can worry about the rest."

Dusting himself off he reached into his back pocket, retrieving a piece of well-worn lined paper.

"This," He continued, indicating the page in his hand, "is a map of the cellars, there is a tunnel out."

"Why didn't you take it *in*?" asked Grace shaking her head at his stupidity while remembering the guard jumping him on the front step, "It would have saved you time, and gotten you past at least *one* of the guards." She joked, still whispering, careful of being overheard.

"Because, it only works one way, all the gates are locked from this side." Ethan answered rolling his eyes. Grace had always underestimated him. He passed the crumpled page on to her. "Keep this, and look it over carefully. If we get separated, move on without me, I *will* catch up. Okay?"

"It's a deal." Grace responded, looking the page over. She traced the lines in the dim light, looking for the cellar.

Grace located the cellar on the page, looking up to find the corresponding mark etched into a pillar not far from the one Ethan had been tied to. He continued to rummage through his pockets desperately, searching for whatever else he had left with him.

Walking quietly towards the pillar as quickly as she could, she read the instructions carefully relying on the diagram to compensate for her poor reading skills. At each checkpoint there would be a mark and under it a lock.

The code read: *one, seven, nine, three, five, two*. Grace repeated the numbers under her breath, memorizing them. She looked below the mark on the pillar, finding a dial tucked into the wooden post. It looked like a fancy upside down triangle, scrolled delicately to look like angels wings. She turned the dial to the number one and gave it a little push in.

It gave way almost immediately, sinking a section of the floor into a ramp leading down. Piles of debris shifted loudly as they slid into the cavity. Clouds of dust billowed up smelling of rot and years of waste. Grace covered her ears at the blast of noise as the debris crashed to the bottom of the incline.

"We need to move fast." Ethan warned, "The guards must have heard that."

Quickly shifting through the piles of falling boxes and chunks of wood, he disappeared into the ground.

Grace was quick to follow, carefully pulling the dial out and twisting it away from the one, before diving into the tunnel. The ramp slowly rose up behind her crunching to a halt as it caught on the crates and pews that had slid down. The sound was loud enough to be heard from the street, leaving a dull ringing in her ears.

ESCAPE

Grace began to run, trying to put as much distance between her and the noisy opening as she could muster before the guards came and caught her. The dark was overwhelming and disorienting, the air damp and musty. It smelled of something that could only be described as old.

Parts of the path were damp and muddy on her bare feet, others slick and hard as if sections were made of stone. The uneven terrain slowed her and she stumbled on blindly through the pitch and roll of the tunnels below the church basement, feeling as though she were running into purgatory willingly.

To her, anything would be better than the hell above her.

Grace had been accustomed to dim lights, after all those years in the tower her eyes were familiar with adjusting to the darkness around her. The tunnel however, remained dark, even to her. Grace found her hand a wall to run along and relying on touch and smell alone, she continued moving at a relatively fast pace through the tunnel. She breathed steadily as her feet paced along the tunnel.

She pretended it was the route to the police station she had been practicing alone in the tower. Even unseeing, it felt nice to know that she could walk in a straight line for more than three paces before walking into a wall. She could feel the damp creeping up her pant legs with each puddle she stepped in as it seeped through the thin fabric, absorbing it up like a sponge. The walls were dripping and she had bumped her head on a low rock, leaving it throbbing mildly. She timed her footsteps with the pulsating pain to keep herself going. She was in a hurry to put a distance between her and the church.

***

Ethan waited for Grace to enter the tunnel. He watched her duck in as the ramp tried to return to the cellar floor. He covered his ears at the loud crunch of the rubble being pinched in the entrance as it tried to close over again. The tunnel grew dark. Noises sounded further in over the ring in his ears, probably animals, thought Ethan.

He waited a moment longer, thinking his eyes would adjust.

"Grace?" He whispered, hoping she could still hear after the deafening crunch of debris. "Stay close, I have a light." He continued, optimistic that she was listening to him somewhere in the dark.

He couldn't waste any time waiting around. Soon the guards would be rushing down and with the entrance still open slightly, they were sure to know where Grace and their captive had disappeared to.

Ethan reached into his pocket and removed a small flashlight that the guards had overlooked. The light from it was dim and quickly absorbed into the darkness of the long tunnel. It cast an eerie green cloud into the tunnels thick air. He looked around for a moment, searching for Grace in the light.

"You already left, didn't you..." He mumbled into the darkness, disappointed that she hadn't waited for him. Looking forward, his light didn't capture Grace anywhere ahead in the tunnel either. He began to move quickly, hoping to catch her.

The path was difficult, his shoes caught in the mud making suctioning noises when he pulled them out. He tried moving faster to avoid sinking in, stumbling twice where the deep mud became stone slab raised slightly higher as the softer areas had sunken in over time.

Ethan was not a very athletic kid. He had never played any sports, so keeping a steady fast pace was tiring on him. If his life had not depended on his escape, he would have stopped for a break. Adrenaline was kicking in, giving him an edge as his senses became familiar with picking out obstacles within the tunnel. He hoped he would catch up to Grace soon. He worried that he might have passed her. Every couple of minutes he would whisper, "Grace..." to see if she was close enough to hear him.

Ethan's shoes were filling with water. He felt like he was walking in a swamp as muck sloshed around inside his socks. He wished he had thought to dress better for the excursion. He should have packed something warmer for Grace too. Underground the air had a damp chill to it that was pleasant against his flushed skin while he worked up a sweat walking. Soon, however, the cold air would be a problem.

Grace was only wearing thin layers and could easily catch a chill or pneumonia from the exposure in the passageway and he needed to get her out alive.

TUNNEL

Grace moved quickly, cautiously testing her footing with each step after almost falling over what was probably a tree root. She made her way through the tunnel hoping that there would be no fork in the road along the way. With no light, she couldn't check the map Ethan had given her. At every support beam Grace would pause, quickly pushing a hand in front searching for a wall before her, afraid of walking into it head on. She was disappointed a little bit more each time she swiped her hand through the air and felt nothing in front of her.

The tunnel inclined slowly, growing steeper as Grace moved on. Downwards it grew danker and darker. The air was almost too thick to breath. Like soup it caught in her lungs making it harder to press forward.

Grace pushed on determined to make it to the next checkpoint before the guards caught up. She knew the entrance to the tunnel was still passable with the junk caught up in the opening preventing it from closing safely behind them. It was a dead giveaway as to where she and Ethan had disappeared to. With all of the commotion the moving floor had caused in the cellar they would have to be incompetent not to realize they were down that hole in the floor.

She was wondering how far behind they were when her foot slipped from under her. It sent her sliding down a wet hill and it took her a moment of fumbling to regain her footing. She was covered in mud and sweat, lurching forward through the soupy muck, ankle deep in parts. As the caked mud began to dry on her arms and back in a breeze from below, she became uncomfortable and cold. The drying mud cracked on her skin as she moved.

Behind her a dim light bounced against the ceiling as it ambled along like a humble green cloud in the distance. She quickened her pace and it began steadily growing farther away, but she would not let up until she was through the checkpoint and had closed it behind her. She hoped the guards had not caught up to Ethan. He was surely somewhere behind her, he hadn't kept pace and when she whispered his name no one answered. She hoped he would catch up soon.

She would wait for him on the other side of the checkpoint. Surely the guards wouldn't know how to get beyond it. She could rest while she waited, knowing that she was finally safe. The thought pulled her through as her foot became suctioned, stuck in the thick soup of goop beneath her.

***

Back in the church's great room the guards turned, looking to one another with confusion as a loud crash shook the decaying floorboards beneath them. Pieces of angels fell from their pewter holdings in the boarded up windows, crackling across the room with an eerie twinkle as they shifted across the floor towards Steve and Walt's feet.

"Was that the storage room?" Asked Walt, looking to his companion with confused bewilderment.

The hostage was down there and it felt like he was bringing the rest of the church down with him. The floor shook again with more force. From beneath the floorboards a sound like shattering wood resonated through the church. It was as if hell had opened up beneath them. Walt was suddenly fearful. Remorse swam through his veins as he deliberated.

"Yeah, we'd better both go." Steve looked terrified at the thought of going back into the dark cellar again to discover what that unearthly noise was.

Stepping over the broken coloured glass carefully he lead the way to the staircase, deliberately choosing his footing carefully to stall, hoping Walt would take the lead.

The guards ambled grudgingly down the flights of stairs and into the cellar slowly with their weapons drawn. Walt had never fired a gun in his life. His hand shook as he held the tip of the gun away from his face, safety still on. It was more for intimidation than anything.

With their flashlights out, the two circled the wrecked room together looking for their captive. All they found was an empty post and a sinkhole in the floor. The two stopped short of the opening, cautious of the floor giving way beneath them.

"What's this?" Walt looked at the sunken floor and the shifted boxes. He pointed his light at a pew caught in the gap, half splintered from the force. The dust had settled back down, but the stench of rotting damp earth was pungent and stifling in the confined space of the cellar. It clung at the hairs on the back of Walt's neck as he realized what was happening.

He should have read the manual when he had taken the position as a guard at the church. Something was in the basement, he just couldn't remember what. Looking at the damage the sinkhole had caused to the crushed boxes and rubbish, he was sure it was nothing good.

Steve pointed his flashlight at the opening, leaning into it to take a look at the dark crevasse beneath, "Look Walt, it's a tunnel!" He exclaimed.

In the confusion he confirmed that he had not read the manual either, "They must have left together through there…" Steve paused, circling his flashlight over the hole "…I'm calling this in." He trailed off reaching for his cell as he tucked his light back into his belt.

"Do we follow or wait for backup?" Walt asked before Steve had a chance to get his phone out of the pocket he was struggling with.

"I'll call it in, they'll probably tell me to do that anyway…" He trailed off as his phone came free of the tight breast pocket he had slipped it in that morning.

Steve walked away to the stairwell looking for a signal. He glanced over his shoulder at Walt, worried about leaving him alone in the cellar. If the girl and her fugitive were capable of that much destruction, he wasn't sure how far they would be willing to go to get out of the church.

She *was* a criminal after all.

Walt waited at the entrance to the tunnel, keeping his light trained on the opening as he listened intently for any sounds of movement in the cellar. He was not fully convinced that they had even entered the chasm. It could just as likely be a trap for him and Steve to stumble upon. They were probably looming in a corner waiting for Steve to return so they could shove them in and close the ground back up, leaving them lost forever.

Walt looked over his shoulder cautiously, jumping at the sound of Steve walking back towards him after several minutes of silence.

"Called for backup." Steve said struggling to replace the phone in the tiny chest pocket of his uniform shirt, "I say we follow, both of us. Just until backup gets here." He stopped to pull his flashlight back out, clicking it on with gusto, "At least it will look like we tried." He smiled to Walt knowing that neither of them wanted to face the girl anyway.

Walt waited while Steve adjusted his holster, checking his gun clip just in case he needed it in the tunnel. Walt looked for an opening big enough for them to fit though. He crawled down shining his flashlight looking for lights, listening for sounds.

When Steve joined him he knew they were too far behind to catch up.

They trudged on anyway, knowing the consequences if they did not follow were worse than a walk through a murky tunnel.

HIDDEN

Ethan slowed his pace, looking frantically with his dim light from side to side. He hoped to see Grace paused for a break. He secretly worried that he had passed her already. He knew as a child she had been filled with energy, but after years of captivity he was concerned about her keeping up and ahead of the guards that were likely soon to follow.

He was exhausted and having trouble breathing in the damp warm air. His breathing became heavier as the tunnel dipped further into the earth and his lungs burned from exhaustion. The air grew staler and thicker the farther in he went. Ethan could not breath, pausing to catch his bearings he dared turn his light off for a moment to conserve the battery life. He held his hands over his head to open up his airway, a trick he had learned as a child to help overcome severe asthma attacks. He crouched on the balls of his feet, taking deep painful breaths trying desperately to stifle off an attack.

The guards had frisked him before tying him against the post in the cellar, his inhaler had been chucked somewhere in the piles of boxes surrounding him. He may have had a backup in the messenger bag of supplies he had toted in over the wall, but the contents had been spilled in a trail over the front steps and across the church floor. It was empty before they had reached the winding staircase. He knew he should have chosen a more secure bag for the supplies. Now scattered out of reach, he wasn't sure they would have all the necessary tools to get through the tunnels.

As his breathing calmed, Ethan heard noises in the tunnel behind him. It sent his heart racing in a panic. Standing quickly, he turned back to look and noticed that the tunnel was growing brighter like a train coming towards him with its high beams on. The lights were bright and numerous. Someone had a light and was following up behind him.

It confirmed his hopes that Grace must be ahead of him, Ethan rose and continued on in the dark. He tucked his flashlight back into his pocket leaving it off, not wanting to give away his location. He tripped forward catching a face full of the putrid mud that infected the tunnel floor. The path was more intense than he had anticipated. More like an obstacle course than a gateway and without the light of his flashlight he was unfamiliar with the loss of his sense of sight. He only hoped that he could make do without it long enough to evade the guards closing in behind him, once they spotted him it would be over and both he and Grace would be dead. Rising from the slick muck he began forward at the fastest pace he could manage as his feet caught and he tried to rely on his other senses.

***

Grace, with one hand grazing the wall beside her, came to a halt as her other hand finally made contact with something solid. With two hands she felt the stones in front of her and began searching for a dial. A grin spreading across her face as she realized that she was finally close enough to safety to relax in a moment, just as soon as she got the dial set.

Heavy breathing was growing closer, Grace paled as she felt her safety slipping away. She traced the wall frantically searching for the dial until finally her hand made contact with the circular protuberance. She started spinning it wildly, hoping to land on the right number by luck as she randomly stopped it trying to push in before resuming with spinning again.

ESCAPE

The breathing was right behind her. She froze in the middle of a spin of the dial as something hit the wall heavily beside her.

"Ugh…" Ethan groaned as he fell beside Grace with a heavy slap.

"Thank goodness it's you and not the guards, I see you have finally caught up…" Grace chided breathing out heavily as she calmed down from the excitement, "I can't find the numbers on the dial." She pointed to the wall, not realizing that Ethan couldn't see her in the dark.

Ethan stood, blushing in the dark cavern. He was almost glad for the lack of light as he reached into his pocket and retrieved his flashlight. Clicking the button, he squinted, his eyes adjusting to the dim light again. Grace blinked twice quickly to clear her eyes as she frantically turned the dial to seven and pushed it in with as much force as she could muster.

With a slight clicking noise the wall began to lift before her. She watched as it disappeared into the ceiling leaving only a foot of the original wall dangling with the dial sticking out near the top. Grace ducked under swiftly, stepping over the gap in the floor where the wall had sunken in leaving a deep trench swelling with water from an underground stream.

"Switch it back off." She whispered to Ethan urgently, watching as light approached from the distant hollow of the tunnels.

Ethan reached up pulling the dial back out and giving it a quick spin before diving under the wall. He nearly got caught in the trench under it. Luckily the wall was slow moving or he would have been one foot short of a pair as his sneaker caught perfectly in the groove. Slowly the wall lowered back to the ground with a damp click, sloshing stale water at them in a shallow wave when it locked in place.

Taking a quick break on the other side of the wall, Ethan and Grace relished in the fact that they were finally safe from the guards. Slowly their hearts settled back into a natural rhythm as the pressure and terror of the situation died back down to a simmering roar.

From there on out, they could take their time as long as they made it out before they starved that was. Ethan couldn't help but feel guilt at the fact that they were travelling without supplies and he was unsure of what the trek ahead of them held. All the research he had done had been ambiguous.

The tunnels were said to be a myth and the books that had acknowledged them as fact had little to no information regarding their magnitude. They were running blind with nothing to carry them though. Although he was worried, he couldn't let on to Grace just how dire their situation was. She needed to have hope. She didn't deserve more to worry about, so Ethan kept his lips sealed.

"How long is this maze?" Grace asked, looking around the small opening they had entered.

"My source said it could take a while, I had supplies...but…" He trailed off apologetically, realizing that she was worrying about the length of the tunnel, it was like she could read his thoughts. He smiled at her through the dim green glow of his flashlight as it glowed around them.

"Shouldn't be too bad…" He added, trying to lighten up the situation by being cheerful.

"Hey, don't worry about that..." Grace began, chuckling lightly when Ethan held the light at his chin making a goofy face into the beam as it shone across his face. The light etched in strange shadows that gave him the look of a ghoul, childish, but she had missed his humour. Grace continued to stare at him as he spoke to her softly, bringing the light between them brightening them both up like they were in a bubble of light together in the dark of the earth.

"I was supposing to charge in like a knight in shining armour to save you from your tower…" Ethan began quietly. "It was suppose to be chivalrous you know." He raised a brow, looking up into Grace's smiling dirt covered face.

Grace chuckled, "Ethan, you are ridiculous." She concluded, giving him a light shove in the chest. She was so relieved to finally have someone to talk to, she couldn't stop smiling. She pulled him in for a hug, knocking the light tumbling ahead of them into the tunnel. She missed the look on his face as she embraced him tightly for a moment before he darted ahead to catch up with the flashlight, heart pounding.

The path continued on through a series of winding tunnels. Low ceilings in stone arched caverns left them crawling through sections and kept them on their toes, awaiting new obstructions and challenges along the way. Collapsed walls sent them climbing over debris just as they had gotten accustomed to the falling arches at their sides.

Along the walls in even intervals were candles in delicate brass hinges, most looked as if they hadn't been used in hundreds of years. Cobwebs clung to the dry wax drips, dangling from the holders as though the candles had burned through unobstructed by human life. It was like they were left to warn those who chose to use the tunnels after their purpose that it had once been a place busy with life. Names carved into the wooden pillars decayed into gibberish, crumbling as the lives they represented had long forgotten that place.

Gloom crept through Grace when she wondered if anyone had ever been trapped in there, not knowing the next number in the sequence, stuck forever in a forgotten maze. She shuttered and stopped looking down, just in case she came across a straggler.

Ethan was struggling as his shoes caught in the rubble. Sopping wet, they squelched when he took steps, slipping on rocks and catching in crevasses. Grace, barefoot, seemed to have better luck scaling the small mountain. She brushed carefully under the ceiling and down the other side. Her feet were cracked and peeling from the mud, slowly drying in layers and falling off. The walls were dangerously unstable in the section they were in, providing little support to the drooping ceiling. Grace and Ethan hurried through with desperation to find someplace safer to slow down.

"What were these tunnels for?" Grace asked, curiosity finally taking precedence over her silent struggle with the pile of debris laid out before her.

"Back in the civil war," Ethan huffed, keeping up so he could keep his voice low, "They were a safe way for the Southerners to escape with their family through the church...not everyone got to pick their side.." He scoffed at the dampness.

"Kind of like you and I..." He trailed off darkly, covering it up with an awkward forced laugh.

Grace bit her lip, imagining the families fleeing through the same dank tunnels searching for their freedom like Ethan and her. Struggling through the tunnels like their very lives depended on it, she could relate and it made her feel even more depressed at the state of the tunnels. The real reason why they were one way; so they could never go back. The thought of leaving a loved one behind and never being able to retrieve them opened up a wound in her heart that she had been healing for years.

It had been forever since her and Ethan, best of friends in private school, had shared secrets with one another. She didn't know how much Ethan knew of her capture and the circumstances surrounding it, only that she was locked up to keep certain things hidden.

She didn't want him to know either. Ethan would hate her if he knew. Maybe he already did. He was the thing she had left behind, never to return to and with no way of turning back. She was not willing to throw away a second chance with him, not for anything.

They walked on in silence for some time. Both were lost in thought while they struggled with the underground terrain looking at it with a strange new understanding. The tunnels were never a happy place to be, anyone that had ever passed through had been running from something. If she was quiet enough Grace could feel the adrenaline of all those who had been chased through before her resonating against the decay, still pulsating now in her veins. The tunnels seemed alive.

Soon she and Ethan had to pause briefly for an awkward washroom break in the already dank tunnels, each taking a turn walking back and away from the light to relieve themselves awkwardly. It was not as awkward as Grace would have thought. Because it was more of a factor in their survival, it became second nature not to talk about it. Ethan thought about it for a while nervously; his attempted chivalry had backfired so dramatically. Not only had she saved him from the villains, but urination in a tunnel reminded him more of imprisonment than freedom; it was embarrassing.

TRACKING

Walt and Steve walked along slowly, lighting the way with their bright LED flashlights bouncing merrily against the rough dripping walls. They had tried to keep a running commentary on the season of football, but it had quickly died out as each would pause to listen ahead too often to bother talking.

The tunnels echoed and the underground noises and echoing movement of their own feet kept them both on guard, wary of the girl and her strange companion. They were prepared for an ambush. When the guards had reached the stone wall they stopped, flashing their lights around looking for an alternate route.

"There is no way they could have gotten past here." said Walt, confused.

He ran his hand over the filthy wall and the lines scratched into the dirt. It looked like fingernails, someone had been there. It looked fresh and even, but he was no forensic scientist, so he kept his mouth closed.

"Well I saw footprints, so someone came down here." Steve huffed to Walt defensively as he scoured the corners for hiding fugitives. He leaned over to squint at a mound of mud with concern, poking at it with his gun until he was satisfied that it was inanimate.

"We should go back and see if there was a fork we missed or

something. I'll watch the walls, you check up for manholes." Walt took charge, shining his light back and forth across the darkness of the tunnel behind them from the direction they had come.

He began walking and Steve scurried to catch up. Light trained at the uneven ceiling, it looked like it would collapse the second someone on the surface walked over it. He hoped they were somewhere remote.

"The boss is gonna kill us." whispered Steve.

"I know…" Walt agreed with a grimace.

They walked slowly, dissecting every inch of the tunnel with their eyes as they trained their lights in the designated directions. They checked for crevasses, exits, alcoves; anywhere their two fugitives could have escaped to. They needed something to save their lives from the inevitable punishment waiting for them at the church.

The path back to the cellar was more treacherous than they had anticipated. Climbing back up the muddy hill was like trying to go up a waterfall. Their feet slid from under them as the cascade of slime stuck to their shoes. The smell of rot clung to their uniforms after they had finally gotten to the top, covered to the knees with the dank stuff. They plodded back to the cellar noisily, their shoes squeaked rhythmically in the hollow echoing back teasingly at their failure.

***

Ethan and Grace had arrived at a dead end, out of breath from the exertion of the broken passage behind them. A rotting iron grate above them sat still, locked only by the third dial. Ethan twisted the lock, cracking through aged rust towards the nine. He twisted his fingers against the sharp rusted edges with effort. It caught at the eight, slicing his index finger against a sliver of rusted metal.

Pushing the dial in caused clouds of dust to pour down on them as the grate shook free from years of silence. It clicked slowly along, protesting loudly as it lowered its left side to their feet providing a ladder up into the abyss. Rocks began pouring from the opening, growing larger and heavier as the grate opened into the space above. Grace and Ethan retreated back into the tunnel as the clacking of cascading rocks peaked and then slowly dwindled off into a ringing silence.

Grace considered for a moment that the tunnels might be booby trapped to prevent unwanted strangers from sneaking through. Surely if the South had used it to escape, they would have worried about the North following? Taking a deep breath she walked to the hill of stones, wary of her footfalls. She would have to watch her every step carefully.

More rust broke free while Grace climbed. Her palms were bleeding from the rough edges and her cracked feet were wearing no better against the new element. At the top she ducked into the small tunnel using Ethan's flashlight to look ahead while she waited for him. She crawled forward to give him room to climb up behind her. The space was small and she was hunched onto her knees, trying to press against the wall enough to leave him a spot. He finally reached the top, moments before the grate slowly clicked back into place shaking up more clouds of rusty dust into the air. Grace smiled to Ethan, tucking the flashlight between her teeth she turned and started forward.

Grace twisted herself into the opening head first, hoping it would widen out on the other side. The disappointment was familiar to her while she slithered along gaining ground slowly. The flashlight knocked at her teeth as it shuttered against the circular tunnel walls. She felt claustrophobic as the confinement continued, the silence broken only by the scraping of their bodies and the heaviness of their breaths.

The air was cooler in the new tunnel section, dryer. Ethan was able to keep up to Grace's pace, pulling himself along in an uncomfortable crawl. He hoped the tunnel would open up soon. The rough edges pulled at his clothes, tugging when he pushed forward. He had already ripped his shirt in a couple of places, scraping the skin underneath in the process.

Grace carried the light in her mouth clutched firmly between her teeth. The metal was cool against her already cold lips. The chill of the tunnels had already slipped through her thin clothes and was slowly making its way to her bones. She fought to keep her teeth from chattering afraid she would lose their only light. Pulling herself along the tunnel rapidly, she could feel her freedom only three more doors away. She bit the end of the light at the scrapes on her knees, wincing at the sound of metal against her teeth. Dirt was rubbing into her cuts as the tunnel grew smaller. Her tattered clothing thin and damp, rubbed against her skin like wet sandpaper scraping her skin raw. Grace and Ethan moved along on their stomachs, gripping the rocks to pull them forward silently.

Ethan could feel his arms falling asleep from the awkward position. His shoulders ached in protest, having already been tested to their limits earlier that day when the guards had dragged him down the stairs. He worried about Grace being in front. The thought had occurred to him that the tunnels could be rigged to prevent travel and the rocks that had fallen on them were surely a sign of things to come. Pulling himself forward on his stomach his shoulders cramped, slowing him for a moment as he re-adjusted in the confines of the brick tunnel.

The rescue had become a living nightmare. The more he thought about it, the more guilt he felt. He knew that although she hadn't complained once, Grace deserved better than this. She deserved fanfare and cake and a castle far away from the evil dragon that had kept her hidden from the world, *if only real life were that easy*, he thought bitterly.

"I... need...a...rest..." Ethan panted after nearly an hour of scraping along. His elbows were bleeding openly and he thought he could hear his bones scraping against stone.

"Just for a minute," Grace garbled, "It's got to get bigger soon, then we can rest longer." She replied around a mouth full of flashlight.

She stopped and rested her chin on the cold stones, arms going limp as she panted through the tunnel. It echoed back like someone was watching them in the darkness ahead.

Ethan collapsed into a rubbery mess of aching muscles not moving as he listened ahead for Grace. He tried to determine how she was doing with this long strenuous escape after years of solitary confinement. He worried that he was pushing her to go too far too fast.

***

Steve and Walter had reached the sinkhole at the entrance of the tunnel, baffled. They had paused at every bump in the trail. Searched for hiding places or escape routes and had found none. They were filthy, cold, wet and terrified that they had just come up empty handed. They stopped for a minute, flashing their lights every which way hoping to catch a glimpse of something before they had to face him.

"You will need the code to proceed." A husky and cruel voice outside the opening spoke.

"Sir." Walt acknowledged, jumping at the voice. He wondered just how long he had been up there watching them. "The tunnel ended, they weren't in here." He insisted, trying to sound professional like he was of value. His only hope was that the desperation in his voice hadn't translated across to the surface; the other guards said he could smell fear.

"You will need the code to proceed. Six checkpoints. Most are dials." Responded the voice sternly as though he was biting back his anger that the two guards had not known this. "And bring them back alive." He continued, snarling as he tossed a small duffle through the opening. He kicked the last crate holding the opening down into the tunnel sending the ceiling moving back up towards the cellar floor.

It shuttered to a halt, closing the two guards in as a shower of debris fell on them from above.

"Shit." Muttered Walt.

Walt and Steve had never met their boss face to face but they could tell from his tone that they were in deep shit when he locked them into the cavern under the church.

"This is going to be a long night." He mumbled to Steve.

***

He had always known that girl was feisty, with a fiery passion that matched her raging red hair. He had anticipated that she would try to flee, and had warned the guards to look for signs. But he had not expected her to have a helping hand with her escape and he had certainly expected his hired staff to be more punctual with her capture. Their incompetence was astounding, she had managed to single handily evaded them while her accomplice had been tied in the cellar waiting.

The tunnel, a feature Hart had enjoyed with the purchase of the church, had been a clever means of moving the girl should anyone send inspectors to his cover up church re-habilitation project for an inspection. Luckily the inspection was something that had yet to occur in the years that had passed since the original purchase of the property when he had agreed to the restoration of the church. To have his own tunnel used against him was infuriating. He would not rest until the intruder had felt his wrath.

"The wrath of a wealthy man is a horrifying thing indeed…" He mused to himself, chuckling into the damp cellar air. He could hear his guards scurrying away from him into the tunnel like scared rats. Rolling his shoulders back, he turned from the cloud of dust rising from the spot where the floor had shifted and marched up the spiral stairs into his dilapidated room of angels.

FLOOD

Grace and Ethan had continued through the tight crawlspace and emerged in a vast anteroom, falling from the tunnel in a pile on the cold stone floor. Every wall looked the same and asides from the hole in the wall where they had entered, there appeared to be no escape.

It looked like a dead end.

Grace flashed the light on the four corners and across the ceiling with no sign or clue to tell them what direction they should be going. They were sealed in like a tomb, with only one exit visible, the way they had come in.

Grace knew that even if they did turn around, they would be stuck at the grate. The tunnels were designed to go only one way. She looked around for others, worried that the whole thing was a trap and that they had reached the end of the rope. Her breath caught in her throat as the familiar feeling of claustrophobia crept up on her. If they *were* stuck in a trap, at least she was not alone, and that was enough to calm her down.

She reached for Ethan. His hand fell light against her palm. As he wrapped his fingers in hers he gave her a reassuring squeeze, she knew then that they would be alright.

"Well, is this a checkpoint?" Grace asked Ethan while reaching for her map to check.

She held his hand a moment longer, before letting go to hold the light up to see. When she flashed light on the wet muddy page that had been held in her drawstring the rest of the room fell into darkness around her.

"It should be." He replied looking around in the dark for a clue, "I guess we just find the dial now." He walked away from Grace, his feet squeaking sharply on the smooth stonework of the floor.

Ethan began searching the farthest wall, feeling every crevice and relying on touch rather than sight. Grace still held the light, faced downward at the filthy page she was trying to decipher. She looked over the sheet of paper, trying to see the anteroom through the mud smears and water spots.

She frowned. The page was almost useless, it was so ruined from the earlier parts of the tunnel; *one, seven, nine, three, five, two.* She repeated in her head, keeping the numbers in the front of her memory. She knew the piece of paper she held couldn't get her to the end of the maze.

Disappointed, she moved to another wall looking and feeling carefully for a fourth dial. She returned the sheet of paper to her waistband mechanically, it was probably useless now.

***

Steve and Walter had been looking through the duffle bag, trying to make heads or tails of it. It contained chloroform, a cloth, dried fruit, zip ties, water, batteries and a rather odd map.

Walter had already replaced all of the items back into the duffle, save the map which Steve was poring over. Their boss had always seemed like a mysterious man, who else would hire someone to guard one prisoner when the county jail was only three blocks away. He also paid them more than the guards at the state penitentiary and although they had never questioned it they understood that she was more dangerous than he let on. And now she was on the loose.

The supplies he had left them with to catch Grace and that boy from the cellar were bizarre, but Walt trusted that their boss knew what he was doing.

"That wasn't a dead end…" Steve concluded holding the long scroll of thick parchment up for Walt to see. Flashing his light against the yellowing page, he could see the intricate scrolls of ink intertwined in delicate swirls and loops. Someone had put great detail into this map of underground tunnels. It was so beautifully drawn out it could be framed and put up on a wall.

In fact, looking closer, Walt realized that this was the very same image he looked at every day. Hung up across the wall from him every day was a print of this map and he had never taken the time to notice. He shook his head in frustration.

"Looks like we're turning around again." Walt spoke dryly into the echo of the tunnel hoping that Steve wouldn't pick up on the familiarity of the map.

"Yup, this is going to take a while." Steve folded the ageing parchment back into a neat square and tucked it into his back pocket for safe keeping. It seemed he and Walt were going to be stuck together for a while.

Walt huffed as he turned and began trudging back through the tunnel towards the stone wall. He was so sick of his job and the strain it caused his real life, the one outside the church walls. Besides, his wife was going to kill him if he missed another dinner. The hours here were atrocious; but his boss was *really* going to kill him if he didn't bring Grace back in one piece. He trudged on bitterly wishing he had finished college and gotten a real job like everyone had told him to.

The ground was thick with sludge; it clung to their boots like a paste and smelled of clay and mould. Evenly spaced were the wooden pillars that appeared to keep the decaying walls from crashing down. Walt could see the beams rotting though in damper sections, giving way to the acrid smell of the underground prison that Hart had condemned them to.

Footprints sunk deep in the hill of muck, clearly marking the path of the runaways and their own previous attempt at catching up to them. Steve shone a light at the wall tracing the lines left by Grace's hand as she had followed along. She had left a line of scratches in the pliable surface of the rotting clay wall.

The two guards moved like snakes on their second run through the tunnel, sliding in silent unison through the thick damp tunnel with a prey and a purpose.

***

Grace and Ethan had searched every inch of the four walls surrounding them. Ethan now sat pouring over the map with the dim light while Grace paced about the room in a panic, searching every wall over and over again, hoping to find the thing they had missed. She timed her pace by the dripping of water from the ceiling. Slow and calculated, each drop landed with a resonating ping quickly seeping into the floor and disappearing. She hadn't found a puddle yet, nor had she found the dial.

"Grace, hey." Ethan started, breaking the silence.

"Did you find it?"

"It's not a dial, only the first two were"

"Well, what is it then?" Grace whispered angrily. Growling with agitation she scoured the room again briefly, looking for something that was not a dial.

"I don't know. But it's not a dial."

"Great." Grace mumbled resuming her pacing as her words echoed back across the alcove.

A loud click sounded as Grace changed her course. She paused, startled by the sudden noise and the stream of water that came from the ceiling, splashing loudly against the stonework. It smelled of decaying fish carcases. She jumped back from the sound, landing on Ethan as she tripped over his foot. They sat for a moment in a pile on the floor startled at the rush of water, worried that they had fallen into another trap.

"Try that again." Ethan suggested after a moment.

Helping Grace up, he stood, walking towards the dripping water excitedly. He glanced around to see if anything had changed, hoping for an exit door to magically appear. Flashing the light around the room expectantly he came up with nothing.

Grace re-traced her steps with no success. She tried again and again, and then *click*, water rushed from the ceiling in a cascade of decaying stench. She held her foot still although startled by the sudden rush. She looked down and realised the stone her foot landed on was the trigger.

Pressing down harder, she listened as a grinding sound began above. The waterfall grew thicker, filling the room up before it could drain back out. Water crept up to her knees as the smell suffocated them. Ethan trained their light towards the ceiling as a pane of tile slid away revealing a hole through which the torrential amount of water was seeping. The water level rose quickly reaching their knees as the clicking grew louder. A metal ladder slowly lowered from the hole.

Grace kept the pressure steady on the stone, even as her foot began cramping from the awkward pose. The water swam around her waist rising in waves as it bounced against the walls and back. The ladder halted inches from the ground slowly swaying from front to back in the water.

"Quickly." Shouted Ethan as he darted for the ladder. He trudged slowly through the rising water.

The cascade continued to fall into the room. Soon it would be up to her neck. They needed to escape fast.

Grace held her position as he made his way up. The water circled higher, making it to her shoulders with little effort. She shuttered against the cold water and the potent smell it gave off while struggling to keep pressure on the stone under her foot. When Ethan had reached the top he hollered down to Grace over the rush of water.

"Jump on the ladder, it will pull you up."

Grace dove for the ladder, anticipating a quick withdrawal upwards. Instead the ladder slowly clicked back up towards the ceiling leaving her splashing for a few moments too long. She tried pulling herself up a peg, slipping, she almost lost her grip on the ladder.

As water poured over her head, she started to climb falling against the metal rungs with her wet hands and feet. Grace, climbing at twice the speed of the ladders recoil, reached the top long before it had clicked back into place. The pouring water stopped abruptly as the tile slid back to its place. It looked like it had come from a large pipe situated beneath them within the ceiling.

MUSEUM

"Well, you're the expert, where is the *secret* door?" Walt asked Steve sarcastically when they reached the stone wall for the second time that day. He held his light up in anticipation of sudden movement, disappointed that the wall seemed quite ordinary. Maybe Hart *didn't* know what he was talking about.

"Find the dial and I'll show you." Steve stood back cockily waiting for Walt to get to work.

Walt held his flashlight up to the wall and after a few moments Steve began to look with him.

Steve looked the wall up and down with the movement of Walt's flashlight until he saw an anomaly in the stonework sticking out just slightly against the grain of the mortar. A small dial, surrounded by several numbers etched into the stone itself. It would have been hard to see with their light and impossible without one, which meant Grace and her companion had somehow gotten their hands on supplies even after they had frisked the boy down.

"Here." Steve quipped as his fingers found the dial. Twisting slowly he paused on the number one with a slow scraping.

"Now what? Are there magic words?" Walt joked, as they waited for a door to appear. Steve looked disappointed that it hadn't appeared somewhere in the wall. He pulled out his own flashlight, looking at the surrounding area for any subtle changes that he might have missed. The floor hadn't sunk in anywhere and the walls still looked the same. Turning back to Walt at the stone wall, he tucked his light back away.

"That's all it said." He mumbled disappointed at the results, "Three dials, three devices, and a code: one, seven, nine, three, five and two. It should have worked." He looked closely at the dial, tracing the numbers etched into the wall with his finger.

"Are you sure it's on the one and not just near it?" Asked Walt considering something for a moment while Steve checked the dial, "Or maybe the one was for that sinkhole." He observed, remembering how the floor of the cellar had sunken into a ramp that led them into the tunnel.

Steve jiggled the lock a couple of times, turning it to the seven position to test Walt's theory. He paused, hand hovering, waiting for the lock to do something wonderful. Nothing happened. Frustrated, he smacked the lock knocking it in.

"Grrr, stupid piece of junk." He roared into the empty tunnel reaching for the map in his pocket.

The lock clicked in as he hit it. Then the wall began to rise.

***

"It's another storage room." Grace noted, as she and Ethan took in their new surroundings above the alcove of stone.

"Must be deep storage, the locks only work one way." He reminded her, looking around for good measure. He was curious of what would be stored in such an unconventional place, almost like an afterthought.

"Maybe they lived here," She joked looking around at all the clutter piled against the walls, "the cave people…" She whispered ominously into the dark, chuckling at the thought of someone living in worse conditions than what she had come from.

Ethan chuckled overjoyed to hear her laughing.

They walked together shivering from the dampness of their clothing and dripping onto the piles as they stepped over them. As they wound through a short tunnel Grace noticed that it was lined with boxes, brimming with damp disintegrating parchment. Pages stacked in clumps, blocking the path as they decayed.

The smell was stifling, rot and mould mingling in the air. Grace was starting to feel dizzy from all the stale air in the tunnels. It had been hours since she had breathed in fresh air through the tower window, she thought of her own escape route and how she could have been at the police station by now.

Grace reached for a leaf of parchment, curious of the hidden quantity of paper stacked so hazardously along the short hallway at the centre of the underground road that only led one direction. Scrawls of names and dates lined the crumbling wet page printed in old ink, large and delicate. It appeared to be lists of those who had passed through the tunnels over the years. Grace looked around in awe at the piles of disintegrating parchment, likely all covered in names and dates marking the passage of time through the dank walls that surrounded them. The page crumbled as her hand shook from the chill that was seeping through her bones as the dampness of her clothing and the slight breeze started her shaking and chattering.

Soon she was left holding only a corner and Ethan was calling to her to catch up. She raced ahead staying close as he wrapped his arm around her for warmth. He was shaking from the chill nearly as much as she was.

The passage quickly ended with a small room lined with shelves of books. *This is going to take a while*, Grace thought to herself while looking at the scene before her in shock and shivering to the bones under Ethan's arm. He held her closer, rubbing his hand over her arm in a sad attempt to bring some warmth back into her skin.

The library towered over them, nearly twelve feet of thickly lined bookshelves emitting an earthly smell of knowledge into its sealed chamber. The floor was littered with discarded pages and book covers sprawled out spread eagle. It gave the impression that someone was in the middle of some sort of research and had to leave abruptly, leaving remnants of notes tossed across the space.

The otherwise grand library had a look of clutter and neglect. Brass candleholders clung with cobwebs against the walls and bookshelves intermittently. A rotting ladder rose from the depths of a mound of discarded books towards the cathedral ceiling, now crumbling in patches of black mould and cracked plaster. Three walls of treasures lost to the outside world, the sight was overwhelming to Grace.

***

Back in the tunnels the guards had passed the first checkpoint. Quickening their pace with excitement, they wound steadily through the second section, slowing only briefly so Steve could help Walt over the mounds of debris piled up. The path was strenuous on him in his middle age. His joints creaked at the dampness of the pathway like an expectant storm was coming in. He walked stiffly trying to hold his tongue at the pain in his knees. Steve was bearing no better against the underground elements. His skin was slick with sweat and heat rashes had begun spreading down his back and arms making him itchy in his overheated state.

The night was quickly passing, Walt was starving. He stopped and reached into his pockets, searching.

"Here," Steve stopped as Walt pressed something into his hand, "my emergency stash." He joked through a large bite of something out of his own hand.

Steve looked at his hand, smiling. Walt had handed him a granola bar.

Steve was glad for once that Walt had an insatiable appetite. After years of Walt sneaking into his own lunch bag and stealing bites of his sandwich and drinking up the protein shakes they were supposed to be feeding to their prisoner, he had finally pulled through in a bind. He was finally willing to part with his precious food to provide his partner with sustenance to get them out of the tunnels alive, Steve was touched. He unwrapped the bar, bringing it up into the air in a toast.

"Split it?" Steve asked, watching Walt's greedy eyes as he devoured the last bite of his own bar, licking his fingers with satisfaction.

"Nope, I got three. We'll save one for later." Walt confessed seeming smugly proud of himself for making such a diminutive sacrifice, Steve nodded accepting the small offer.

Steve leaned against the wall, sinking in to the slick soft wood of the pillar behind him. He and Walt silently enjoyed a break in the dark tunnels until his radio beeped, coming to life on his belt with a series of flashes and clicks.

"Do you have them yet?" The raspy voice of their boss echoed against the tunnel walls. Steve looked to Walt with horror. Not only had Hart sent them straight to hell for his little prisoner, but now he was demanding speed in the treacherous conditions below ground. It was like working for the devil himself. Steve slowly removed the radio from his belt, holding it an arms distance from his face.

"What do we tell him?" He asked as fear washed over his face; making him even paler in the blue glow of their LED flashlight.

"I'll get this one." Walt responded, taking Steve's radio from his shaking hands. The static cleared as he pressed the intercom, "Sir, we are hot on their trail. Over." He spoke in a professionally monotone voice, wincing at the thought of Hart's displeasure.

"Hurry." the voice demanded. With a click the signal went dead.

"We're dead" Steve whispered in a hollow tone.

Walt nodded, frowning, as they both turned forward and started through the maze once again.

***

Grace and Ethan sifted through the shelves of books, each starting on opposite sides. They were about to pass one another and still no dial or device had been found. They hadn't a clue what they were even looking for in the towering library of lost literature. They had been in the tunnels for over eight hours now and Grace could feel from her exhaustion that they were well into the early morning hours. She stopped as Ethan reached for the same book as her.

"We should rest." She said touching his hand on the bookshelf.

"I know"

He took her hand and stopped to look her in the eyes, noting how her face, even in the dim light, had changed over the years. She looked pale to him, like she hadn't seen the sun since that day in front of the school. She probably didn't even know that he had been standing there, waiting to give her a flower, when the men took her and dragged her away. He hadn't fought them he had hidden behind the tree and waited for help that never came; like a coward. He frowned, guilt welling up in him, guilt that had been eating away at him for ten years.

Ethan led Grace to a pile of books, covered in loose pages. It was far from the entrance and the light breeze didn't reach the alcove, making it seem warmer.

"You rest and then we will continue on." He said bravely, turning to the bookshelf to continue his search as Grace sat down on the pile testing it for uncomfortable protrusions.

"No." Grace said, grabbing for his leg. "We both rest, we're safe. Finally." She pulled Ethan back towards her, gently tugging to sit him down on the heap of manuscripts beside her.

The musty books reminded Grace of the study Ethan's father had let them explore as children. They had poured through his encyclopaedias, learning about the world one picture at a time thinking they were so well educated to be holding the leather bound volumes in their tiny hands like grown-ups. She looked to Ethan, grown to look more like his father over the years than she could ever have imagined.

"How long did you believe I was dead?" She asked softly, thinking back to the image of an eleven year old Ethan weeping by her open grave clutching daisies from their secret garden while they wilted in his trembling hands. She shook violently holding back her tears as she shivered. He wrapped his arms around her snugly.

"Until Jerry and I got the letter." He looked distressed. She could sense the tension in his arms as they broached a topic that was probably difficult for him to think about. "Three, maybe four months ago," he frowned at the recollection, "I felt awful for not coming sooner, but I needed to be sure it was really you, and…" he paused looking ashamed "I needed help."

Jerry had been the Evans' butler and a dear friend of Grace and Ethan. As children they had spent days and weeks alone at the Evans' estate with only Jerry for company. Since both Grace and Ethan's mothers had passed and their fathers worked so strenuously, Jerry had been the only real family either had known.

Grace felt a tug at her chest, "How is Jerry?" She whispered, afraid of how Ethan would answer as he loosened his hold on her.

"Retired." Ethan smiled, poking Grace in the arm playfully, knowing she had been worried about asking, "Plays golf all day now. He stuck by after my dad died, adopted me."

Grace was relieved to hear that Jerry was well. She clutched at Ethan's hand happy that they had at least had each other over the passing years.

"I've missed you." She whispered into the dark as Ethan flicked out the flashlight to conserve the batteries, "And I'm sorry you had to go through so much, I'm glad Jerry was there." She snuggled into Ethan feeling protective of his childhood pain as her drowsiness caught up with her.

"Don't be." He said, brushing her matted hair from her forehead. "You had no one. I can't imagine how that felt"

Grace and Ethan huddled closer, stifling off the cold damp air of the decaying book room. For a few more moments Ethan continued to mumble while Grace fell into a sleeping daze.

With a kiss on her forehead Ethan whispered, "I love you." into the hollow night, before drifting off holding Grace close to his heart.

CHASE

The stonework floor was built in patches, interspersed with sections of gravel that caught Steve off guard. The stone slipped under his feet, sending him reeling when the gravel caught his boots a step later. The walls decayed at his touch when he reached for support. It was like being stuck in a labyrinth from hell he thought, tugging a metal candle hook down on himself.

The whole place felt like a trap made of quicksand. Walt was having less luck. Being a bigger guy, the piles of collapsed stone were proving a daunting obstacle for him to overcome. His feet sunk in farther to the muck puddles that were deeper than they looked. More than once he had needed help retrieving his foot from an awkward predicament. With the help of Steve they remained moving forward, albeit slowly.

The tunnel came to an end at a mound of rocks piled up leading to a grate of sorts, draped across an opening in the ceiling. Walt flashed his light across the area, slowing down so Steve could help him look for the dial. After a few tries they spotted the rusted knob sticking out of the metal grate. Pieces of rust had been chipped off, recently, at least they knew that Grace and her companion were still down there and hadn't discovered a secret way back to the surface yet.

ESCAPE

Walt reached forward taking the dial and giving it a difficult turn to reach the nine. He gave it a sharp tap letting the grate shake debris off onto his hair and shoulders as it clicked into motion, falling slowly into a short ladder up.

They then entered the smallest tunnel Walt had ever seen. It had grown small to the point of restricting. He could barely squeeze his large midsection through parts of the tunnel, slowing their pace to a turtles speed. Walt's belt buckle scraped along the stones with a sickening grinding noise. Steve had taken the duffle bag and was pushing it in front.

Steve was having little trouble, save the squished part, navigating through the opening.

"Go ahead." Walt huffed, as Steve stopped ahead of him in the tunnel waiting. "Wait for me at the end. Yell back when it gets bigger." He wheezed, coughing loudly as his head knocked against the top of the tunnel tapping a stone loose onto his back. He flinched at the pain, hoping that nothing else fell on him and he hadn't collapsed the tunnel by bumping its delicate framework with his head.

"I'll let you know when it gets easier." Steve agreed, worried about his co-worker and long-time friend. He scooted ahead shuffling quicker through the small opening. Soon the tunnel became more passable and he quickly popped out into the opening ahead landing on his shoulders as he rolled across the stone floor to catch himself. He hadn't expected the tunnel to end so abruptly.

"Hey," he called back with excitement, "you're almost there!"

"Keep talking." Walt groaned from inside the tunnel. The scraping sounds grew closer, echoing against the walls while Steve waited for him in the anteroom.

Steve thought for a minute. He wanted to encourage Walt to pull himself through without making him think too hard. He worried that the stress was already too much on him. "Did I tell you I bet on that Titans game last night? I won fifty bucks on it." He chuckled to himself knowing that he had picked the right topic when he heard Walt grumble through the tunnel.

***

Four more men had arrived at the church. The first group of two had already searched the cellar and main floor extensively. The six then split into two groups of three and separated. One group headed up for the tower, the other for the invaders point of entry; the wall.

The first crew trudged up the winding stairs, their heavy feet loud against the warped wooden floorboards that creaked in protest. They followed their captain Roy Mulligan, who had been one of the first two to arrive on the scene. Mulligan was usually on switch shifts with the guys, he was a ground level guard. Mostly because he didn't want to go anywhere near the girl, she gave him the willies. Who would need to be locked up all alone like that, unless they were very dangerous?

He had heard stories about that girl from some of the older guards that had since retired. Story was she was a bad seed, a killer, that's why she needed to be kept alone and guarded twenty four seven by a team. Look at what she had accomplished; they were saying she had nearly killed Steve on her way out of the confines of her tower. He kept his men between himself and the door, just in case she was lurking somewhere near.

"Boys, this is a tricky one." He announced, preparing to tell them the back story Hart had arranged. Knowing which information was vital and what was important enough to be kept under wraps was part of his training as the first on the scene. "Prisoner escaped, looks like it had outside help. You see anything suspicious, report it to me. Got it?"

"Yes Sir." Replied the two in unison, staring at their commanders back. *Perfect,* thought Mulligan. Now they would do all the work for him and never have to know about the psycho lady that was kept at bay in the tower. They would sleep soundly thinking they had helped while he had nightmares of a scraggly red-head killing him in his sleep and burying him in the woods.

Reaching the top of the stairs Mulligan paused on the landing, turning to look directly at his two officers.

"Welcome to the tower." He grinned menacingly as he swung the door open, stepping aside to let his minions in to the cave of the beast.

Within seconds his men had made a discovery. A string of sheets dangled precariously out of the tower window, tied to a bedpost. The pane of tempered glass lay across the room propped against the wall. Mulligan pulled his radio out to notify the other team. He knew that girl was dangerous. He looked around shiftily, hoping she wasn't near. He didn't want her to see him.

He didn't want to be her next target.

***

Walt squeezed out of the opening finally, like toothpaste escaping the tube. His breaths were coming out ragged and laboured as he picked himself up off of the floor. Steve pulled a bottle of water out of the duffle, handing it to Walt encouragingly.

"Let's rest for a minute, this isn't a race." He sat to take a bottle of water for himself.

"Thanks." Walt huffed through heaving gasps. He drank desperately from the bottle, hands shaking. Sinking to the ground, he and Steve sat exhausted, dripping sweat and stuck in a hole leading them to nowhere. With both flashlights flaring across the small space the two could see the room quite clearly.

The floor was damp and a drip from the ceiling left the room with a constant echoing, *plink,* as it hit the stones below. No puddle on the floor meant it was draining somewhere and Walt was willing to bet that was where the exit would be. The map had indicated a number three, but neither one could muster up enough energy to continue searching beyond their wide eyed stares around the room.

It was hard to admit that albeit boring, their cushy jobs had made them soft over the past five years. Normally at this hour they were both indulging in a round of naps outside the tower door after a game of cards.

***

The second crew was walking the perimeter outside the churchyard to the spot where the boy had ventured over the wall the evening before. They paused for a moment at the base of the wall, taking note of the rope coiled on the ground. Looking towards the forest where he had come from. They began back tracking as the sun came up, bringing light to a new day.

A radio buzzed on his belt as his crew tailed behind him on the path "Colt. Check the perimeter, the prisoner may have escaped out the window, over."

Looking back to the church, Colt now saw in the rising dawn a string of sheets trailing in the gentle breeze from the back window of the tower. It was like Rapunzel herself was standing at the window letting her hair blow gently in the morning breeze.

Smart, he thought, it would not have been visible from the front. Pulling out his radio, he responded.

"Checking the perimeter, over." He looked to his team and with a nod, they scattered.

Colt stood by for an extra moment, looking at the tower with wonder. If she had taken the sheet rope down and out then she was probably long gone by now. Was the intruder her distraction, or just a lucky break? Colt was sure Hart had already weighed these options when he arrived on the scene.

His level of agitation had led Colt to believe that the intruder was looking for the girl. But how could she have planned that while locked in a tower thirty feet up and with no contact with the outside world?

***

Mulligan approached Mr. Hart on the main floor tentatively. He was sitting peacefully at the security desk. He looked up menacingly as Mulligan approached.

Mr. Hart was a stern man, set in his ways and Mulligan had learned over the years that he had to be approached in the right manner, no matter what the context or you were likely to lose your fingers. In some more severe cases even a hand or two had been lost at the rage of Hart.

"Sir," Mulligan began boldly to cover his fear. "She may have escaped the tower on her own, the window was tampered with." He continued, standing stiffly with his hands grasped behind his back , palms sweaty.

"Colt and his crew are scouring the grounds for signs." He tilted his head to the ground, waiting for the inevitable blast that always came after giving Mr. Hart news that he did not want to hear.

"How could you have missed that?" Mr. Hart demanded in an even tone that terrified Milligan more than the usual rage he had been expecting.

"It was well concealed…" Mulligan ventured, knowing he was caught in a lie. He looked up hoping to redeem himself, straight into the barrel of a gun.

Mr. Hart had moved soundlessly. The gun shot resonated through the church bringing Mulligan's team through the door, just in time for them to see his body hit the floor.

Mr. Hart sat at the desk, looking up long enough to demand that his men move "faster". He grimaced at the two remaining soldiers as they dragged Mulligan from the room leaving a bloodied trail leading out the front doors.

CLOSER

Walt and Steve had finished off the first two waters. Sitting on the cold stone floor, they had looked around the room twice from their spots, too lethargic to get up. Setting down the light for a moment, Walt noticed something on the floor etched into the stonework

"Hey, flash that here." He asked Steve as he stood from the floor walking to the strange marked stone.

"Okay"

Steve aimed the light at Walt and slowly lowered it down to where he was pointing. A number three was carved into the stone next to him. Walt pressed down quickly. A loud clicking resonated through the room as the flood gates re-opened.

Water poured from the cavity in the ceiling, catching them off guard. Walt shifted his foot, but the cascade continued until the opening had closed completely with an echoing click. Steve had wrapped the handle of the duffle bag over his arms, leaving it clinging to his back as he waded through ankle deep water to Walt's side.

"Well, now what?" He asked, flashing the light to the ceiling he searched for the gap through which the water had been pouring. The water level slowly tapered off as it seeped into the floor. Soon the ankle deep water had become a mere slickness on the stones beneath them.

"We try again," Walt answered, poising to step on the stone once more. "Make sure you get up there first." He added, hoping he would have the time to escape before drowning in the dark cold waters.

Steve nodded, standing directly under the opening. Walt stepped back onto the stone. Water drained into the room and with it the putrid smell of decay and mould. The stream rose up to their knees, slowly taking over their bodies with its cool dampness. As the ladder got closer, Steve jumped, catching hold and scrambling upwards.

***

Grace and Ethan started, awakened by the familiar clicking and the deafening rush of water. They both jumped to their feet, half asleep and terrified that they were about to be washed out again.

"Someone is coming." Grace looked to the hallway as it slowly lit up from a distance. She could see Ethan in the faint light approaching.

Quickly Ethan pressed on his flashlight, running to the bookshelf. "Five, something to do with five..." He mumbled as he searched, tossing books into the growing stack at the foot of the ladder. Grace rushed to his side searching frantically as he muttered to himself.

"Roman Numerals!" Grace exclaimed in an excited hush after several moments of panic. "I think I saw something over here." She dashed to a row of books on the far side of the room. Ethan followed up behind her with the light. Grace pulled at a book with a large golden V on the spine.

The shelves swung back, opening into blackness. Grace and Ethan rushed inside. As the case closed, the lights behind them shut out. They could hear heavy footsteps and yelling from the other side of the wall. It had been a close one, far too close. Grace and Ethan had to make up some time. The guards were hot on their trail and obviously capable of manoeuvring through the tunnels on their own. It was no longer a safe route for them. Their hearts were pounding in protest.

***

Walt and Steve had reached the top of the ladder drenched from head to toe with the slick putrid waste that had been pouring from the pipe hidden in the floor beneath them. Walt was convinced that it had not been water pouring over them in the stone hole. The smell was too raw and earthy for it to be pouring from an underground stream.

It had been a trap.

As they looked down the short, cluttered hall ahead of them, they heard a resonating thud. Looking towards one another, they raced after the noise suspecting they had finally caught up to the fugitives. Walt huffed as he struggled with his belt, trying to retrieve his gun just in case.

Steve passed Walt, racing full speed into the room of books as the case closed with a resonating *click*. "Walt," he called behind him. "We aren't far behind."

He began to search the case, pulling each book out and tossing it to the floor behind him into an already towering pile of pages. Walt quickly scooted in beside him. Taking his lead from Steve, he started grabbing books off of the shelf not even sparing a glance at the titles. They needed to get onto the other side of this bookcase and if they couldn't find the key they had every intention of breaking it down into kindling.

Steve was moving in a frantic frenzy. He was tripping over books faster than he could toss them behind himself. He had watched the bookcase closing against the wall before him. There had to be a trigger there somewhere and it had to be attached to the case in some way. He grabbed at a now empty shelf, tugging it back towards himself hopeful that they could just pry it open without wasting their time looking for a lever. It didn't budge against his fiercest pull, his fingers slipped against the wood and he fell back onto the hard pile that had been growing behind him. Even Walt was working with a desperation that he had never seen before. They were so close and still one barrier away.

TRACE

Colt's crew had searched the grounds thrice, finding only one set of footprints leading in towards the church. After following those out, they discovered they had come from the road on the other side of the woods; it was nearly an hour walk away. Whoever had trekked in that far just to climb a wall into a decaying churchyard had been bound and determined to find something.

It was starting to look quite suspicious as the evidence piled up. Whoever it was on the inside of those church tunnels, they hadn't been a stranger to the situation. Colt considered for a moment; the culprit had been described as a young man.

Colt shook his head at the trees. He walked out of the woods to investigate the side road that the tracks had come in from. A small beaten car sat at the side of the road, with two broken windows and no plates.

Thick scratch marks freshly chipping the dirty brown paint sat under the window frames. It looked as though someone had tried to break in by unlocking the car and after failing had just smashed in the window. Rocks sat on the floor among shards of thick glass. It had probably taken some effort to break in and by the looks of the car it hadn't held anything interesting. It was more likely a local thug had used the car for "practice" for his next real job. *Why not?* Thought Colt, the rust bucket had probably been parked there suspiciously for a while now.

Colt doubted they would get any information out of that source. It had already been ransacked by local teens and probably even reported to the police by other nosy drivers passing by.

He turned back towards the church, glad to have news for Mr. Hart that would allow him to live another day. He felt pity for Walt and Steve, underground in those awful tunnels in the dark, knowing that they would fail.

That would have been him if he hadn't bribed Steve into taking his graveyard shift last night. Instead he had been out for drinks with his buddies when the call had come in. *Get here.* That was all Hart had said. Colt had known, even then, that behind that ominous tone was the threat of death. He had driven drunk from the pub to the church. And he had been sober the second he had laid eyes on Hart, standing like a death omen on the front steps.

Colt wound back through the woods admiring the autumn breeze swirling leaves in small clearings like miniature tornadoes, until a light caught his eye.

He walked to the source, finding a small briefcase tucked under a loose leaf covering. The brass nameplate reflected the morning light, glaring into his bloodshot eyes. It was tucked neatly against the leather trim of the expensive case. Colt dusted off the last leaf flakes as he pulled it from the ground, the nameplate read *"Evans".*

It was then that he realized how much trouble they were all in. His eyes widened with recognition of the family name. Turning to the church, he tucked the case under his arm and ran as fast as he could through the crisp autumn leaves.

***

Grace and Ethan had just narrowly escaped the guards. Standing now at the top of a narrow staircase in the dim light of Ethan's flashlight they paused.

The light was flickering slowly against the walls, wearing through the last of its batteries. Grace felt like she was back in the tower, looking down on her freedom at the bottom of a spiraling staircase. She felt woozy at the thought that she had become trapped at the top again, with a set of stairs standing between her and the rest of her life.

The stairs were damp and slippery under her bare feet. Ethan wasn't having much luck with traction either, falling down the first flight heavily. He bounced the flashlight against the stairs as he crashed loudly into the wall where the stairs turned, crumpling onto the small landing with a loud moan.

"Uuuug." He groaned as he stood fishing for the flashlight he had dropped in the fall.

"Be careful." Grace called as she raced against the slippery steps to catch up to him. Reaching down gingerly, she gave him a hand to grasp as he stood. Ethan swooped back down to grab the light before it went rolling down the rest of the spiral into the oblivion below.

The stairs wound in a zigzag pattern; down towards hell as far as Ethan could tell. They cracked and chipped as they got farther into the section of the maze, causing Grace and Ethan to slow their pace and hold the wall for support.

Grace was cautious of her footing with her raw bare feet. The chips in the stairs left loose fragments of rock that were easily caught under her feet as she moved onto the next step. She had sliced open the arch on one of her feet, adding to the slipperiness of the slick stairs. Pieces of wall crumbled beneath her fingers as she clung to the wall for assistance.

Ethan's feet missed several steps as he raced down the stone spiral, he slipped on patches of wet stone nearly tumbling into Grace who had taken the lead after watching him fall down the first flight. His clumsiness was obviously a trait that he had not outgrown. She hoped that by being in front of him she would be able to catch him before he hurt himself too badly.

Grace paced down the steps, tripping over chips in the decaying stonework. The mud on her soles slipped in patches of dampness. She gripped at the dripping stone walls lightly as they crumbled beneath her fingers. She worried that the slightest touch would send the walls collapsing down around her and Ethan. She was afraid they would be buried alive on the decomposing staircase. Pieces of loose stone clung to the soles of her feet, sticking to the mixture of blood and muck that had accumulated there. It made it difficult for her to continue at a quick pace, she found herself constantly stopping to scrape sharp pebbles off of her feet before they cut her too deep. She was slowing them down and soon Ethan was beside her keeping pace on the narrow stairwell.

"Where does it come out?" Grace gasped, after slipping on a particularly crooked step. She squinted, trying to look farther ahead in the dimness. It was a feeble attempt to find the end of the maze.

"What?"

"Where does the maze end, what's at the other side?" She continued. "Will we be far enough away?"

"Yes." Ethan reassured Grace. "I have a buddy waiting for us. He'll make sure we get away"

"Thanks." Grace panted heavily, catching her breath as she trudged on down the mysterious spiral.

It was impressive how meticulous the craftsmanship was in the maze. Right from the beginning it appeared as though the tunnels had been made for something more than just a route for fugitives. Grace traced the stonework with her toes before stepping onto the next level of the staircase. Someone had worked quite tirelessly to make these stones smooth and level. She tried to imagine the series of tunnels back when they had been first unveiled. With the brass candleholders lit it would have been almost beautiful in its own horrific way.

The stairs abruptly ended leaving Grace and Ethan face to face with another wall. After hours of running and climbing, Grace was ready to collapse. Having had no food or water since her small dinner the night before in the tower, she was famished. She imagined Ethan was feeling the strain too.

"Two..." Grace whispered through heaving breaths. She grasped her waist, suddenly aware of the severe stitch in her side. Ethan began moving the dimming light to search.

Flickering slowly once, the flashlight finally went out. Ethan shook his hand slapping the cylinder against his palm hoping to retrieve some life out of the batteries. It remained dark.

***

Walt had quickly caught up to Steve's fast pace. Working in unison they ripped books from the shelves with desperation that was linked closely with their own desire to live. It hadn't taken them long to find the book that stuck, with the golden "V" etched into the spine Walt had given it a tug intending to toss it across the room, instead it had stuck. Pain shot through his arm at the unexpected reaction when the book hadn't moved as he was anticipating. As the wall swung open he held his elbow tightly to his side, waiting for the numbness to wear off. They slipped through the wall, hopeful that they would catch up in time.

Using both flashlights to compensate for their varying speeds, Walt and Steve trudged cautiously down the stairs with little concern. Their rubber soled work boots prevented the slippery steps from slowing them down.

Walt took up the rear as Steve shot on ahead stopping at intervals to catch his breath, allowing Walt to catch up with him. They couldn't tell from their angle how far down the steps would carry on. Judging by the rest of the tunnels, they paced themselves as though they would be going for a few more hours at the least.

Steve watched the trace marks from Grace's fingertips against the wall, having the same sinking feeling that she herself had had upon seeing the softness of the wall. It felt as though they could be buried alive at any moment. Steve caught his breath, careful not to exhale too heavily. He knew loud noises could trigger avalanches, but he didn't know what might trigger the walls around them to come tumbling down underground.

Walt was heaving from the strain on his body, the farther downwards they travelled the more he perspired. The heat and dampness were too much on his body and he was slowing down to a snail's pace when Steve stopped to check on him.

"Hey, take a break, have some of this." Steve zipped the duffle bag back up at his side, handing over a bottle of water to Walt. "Now would be a good time to have that other granola bar." He added, seeing how pale Walt had become in the dark underground.

He tucked his flashlight into his waist, leaving it on to cast an ambient glow down the stairwell. Walt sat heavily on the step behind him, struggling with the bottle cap as he tugged the melting squished granola bar from his chest pocket.

He was silent as he ate the bar whole, washing it down with half of the bottle of water. Gulping loudly he held the bottle up to Steve, offering him a drink with a slight shake of his hand. Steve shook his head back, seeing that Walt could use the fluid more than him.

There was still one bottle of water in the bag as he slung it back over his shoulder tucking his arms into the handles until it clung to his back like a backpack. Walt finished the water, tossing the bottle back behind him. It rolled down the stairs landing somewhere a few feet upwards.

He stood with effort, rolling his wrist forward to Steve in a silent agreement that they should keep moving forward. He began back down the stairs, passing Steve in his own show of strength. Steve shook his head with a smile, following behind as he tugged his flashlight back from his belt.

ENTANGLED

Colt had reached the church. Bursting through the front doors with the briefcase lifted in his arms like a talisman warding off the evil glances of Hart. He was met by an empty room.

After searching the building, he finally came across one of the guards locked in the tower and tied with the sheet-rope the girl had tried to escape with to her bedposts. As he pulled a portion of cloth from the guard's mouth, he gagged spewing blood across the room.

"Where is Hart? I found something." Colt demanded, slapping some sense into the delirious guard as he untied him from his restraints. The guard struggled against the ropes, avoiding Colt's help as though he were fearful of being freed.

"Left to meet them at the other end…" The lone guard replied through gasping breaths. Blood dribbled from his chin. He looked like he was missing teeth in his bloodied mouth.

Colt finished untying him and he collapsed into a heap on the floor. He could see that blood was also trickling from a wound on the back of his head. He wondered briefly how he had gotten all the way into the tower and tied up. Hart was a very particular man and by the look of the setup he had very little time to get out of there before it became a crime scene.

"Shit." Colt muttered under his breath as he stood quickly, covered in the other guard's blood. He realized he was already implicated in the crime.

Stripping down out of the bloodied clothing, he turned to run from the tower. The door swung closed before he could cross the room. Silence from the other side indicated that he had triggered it from the inside.

Damn Hart and his traps, he thought as he fought against the doorknob. He had to get out of the tower before Hart eliminated them. He turned back to the window, setting his shoulders with determination as he unraveled the roped from the dead guard bleeding out on the floor.

***

Hart sat patiently in the back of his car. One of the three guards he had taken with him was behind the wheel in front of him. He drove at a pleasing pace, sending wind whipping in through the open sunroof at a dangerous speed.

It made it fantastically difficult to breath into the rush of air and the guard beside him was panicking with the struggle. Hart could tell he would be of no use in their future endeavours. He would be removed from the staff pool shortly.

Hart let his mind wander momentarily, imagining the outcome with pleasure. He knew if they wanted to meet the prisoners at the other side they would have to cut a few corners. They sped recklessly through the back country roads and as Hart checked their progress he frowned at the time passing quickly on his diamond encrusted watch.

"Faster." He demanded, shouting over the wind as he reclined back into the plush leather of the back seat.

The driver nodded to him in the rear view mirror, pressing his foot down as the car accelerated forward. Hart's hair whipping into a wild frenzy in the wind as the man beside him struggled even harder to breath. Hart smiled lacing his fingers behind his head he crossed his left foot over his right knee lazily.

"Yes Sir." The driver yelled back over the torrent of wind.

***

Ethan and Grace scratched desperately at the walls in the dark. A light was slowly becoming visible up the stairs, causing Grace to scrape at the wall in a panic. She would claw through the wall if she had to.

Ethan pulled at the bricks beside her, fighting hard to resist the urge to punch the wall in frustration. It would surely break his hand if he did. Instead he followed Grace's lead, feeling the brickwork over in the most obvious spots where a trigger could be concealed; the mortar between the bricks.

He searched for gaps and holes, bricks that might give way like the trigger in the cavern that had filled with water. Nothing seemed to pop out to him and Grace was breathing heavily with panic.

Her fingers were bleeding from clawing at the wall like an animal trying to escape when her finger stuck in a narrow slit. Feeling around with her other hand she found an identical slit beside it.

Noises on the stairs grew closer. Grace shoved her index finger into the slit. Wiggling the two fingers, she triggered a release by pulling down on two levers within the wall simultaneously. Her hand pulled with the wall as it swung open. Her fingers were stuck in the small openings.

"Yes." Ethan exhaled as the wall began to move under his hands. He couldn't see from the angle of the approaching light how Grace had become tangled in the wall. Both of her hands stuck against the moving brick wall and she was tugged forward into the new space.

"Got ya." Exclaimed a voice behind them as the light came into full view.

Two guards grabbed Ethan and Grace from behind. The one holding

Grace fumbled in a bag for a moment, pulling out a handful of zip-ties. Grace was too weak to fight back as they bound her wrists in front of her while she struggled to get her fingers free from the wall. Ethan was quickly held down to have his hands zip-tied together as they dragged him and Grace up against a wall.

***

Walt was relieved, finally they had caught up. Maybe he would live for another day, if Mr. Hart was in a good mood and willing to compromise.

Looking at Grace, he felt pity as guilt rose up in his chest. She looked malnourished and wore scraps of filthy clothing that would be considered rags to most. He and Steve had been responsible for upholding that horrible lifestyle for her and they still had no idea why she was being held captive.

She sure didn't *look* dangerous to him. Her frail petit figure shivered in the wet and cold of the tunnel. Her ribcage was visible through a tear in the fabric of her shirt. He looked to Steve with concern, *should we give her a coat?* He wondered.

The look on Steve's face said *no*.

"Here." He offered her the last bottle of water from Steve's pack. They had reached the other side of the wall safely, watching it click mechanically back into place with a resonating final squish against the thick muck lining the bottom of the doorway. A wave of water splashed against their feet as they stepped out of the large puddle covering most of the floor on their side of the marker.

Grace looked at Walt with disgust. Rundown after all those years imprisoned, her face remained innocent. Walt looked quickly away feeling guilt coursing through his veins again. He sat her down gingerly looking at his hands as he twisted the top of the bottle off, placing it back in her thin hands.

"Drink." He suggested in a gentle voice avoiding eye contact with her, he turned to Steve for support. Steve stood across the tunnel with the boy watching him intently as though he expected him to jump up and attack at any second.

Grace slowly took the bottle to her parched lips, shaking under the weight of the small bottle in her hands. She had devoured nearly half of it before coming up for air, gasping loudly in the awkwardly silent tunnel where she and Ethan had become prisoners.

"Him." She pointed to Ethan. Startling Walt as her demand broke the silence. He looked over quickly, noticing her finger pointing across the tunnel to the boy being held up by Steve on the opposite wall. She pushed the bottle in his direction struggling against her bonds.

Walt took the bottle and passed it to the boy quickly. He was careful not to make any contact with the prisoner, fearful for how cunning he had been getting them into the tunnels in the first place.

He and Steve made eye contact. Both knew the boy would be dead the minute they left the tunnel. Steve locked his eyes with Walt and slowly shook his head at the waste of water. They would not tell Grace, she would find out soon enough.

Steve settled the boy onto the ground. Standing between him and the exiting hatch overhead, he pulled out his radio. He hoped for a signal as he clicked it on. It sent a static ringing through the small space.

"Radio three, over." He tested, as the radio crackled to life in his hands. It filled the small passage way with the static response that lasted for what seemed like forever in the confines of the underground hole.

After a brief pause of static a response resonated, echoing against the walls with crisp clarity.

"Radio three, this is radio one. Name your position. Over"

Grace could feel her body grow cold. She could feel her freedom slipping through her bound hands as he pulled the radio back to his mouth to speak.

Relieved Steve responded, "Last checkpoint sir, we have the prisoner. Over"

The static grew louder as the silence from the other end became unbearable. Walt was beginning to look worried when it finally broke.

"Sit tight until we have secured the exit. Over"

"Understood, over" Steve responded, clicking the radio back to his belt where it rung quietly masking the silence of the tunnel that confined them.

Walt and Steve both looked to the boy. "Who is at the other end of this tunnel?" Steve demanded.

He worried about the other side of the trap door above him. If someone were to open it to check how far the boy and Grace were along, there could be trouble. He looked to Walt trying to convey the thought without tipping the prisoners off. One yell from the boy and he could have backup barging through the small opening to kill them all.

The boy sat still, looking defiantly from Walt to Steve. Quietly smirking, Ethan knew he could make them sweat for a bit. Maybe it was just the distraction he and Grace needed to get out of there alive.

KING

Agent King stood watching a closed trap door, beside him his partner tossed cards at a table lost in a game of solitaire.

King had been with the FBI for six years, partners with Chung for five and stuck in the Kentucky office waiting for his break the whole time. His ambitions would one day take him to Washington, the Pentagon or Area Fifty One. But today he stood watching a hole in the floor, waiting for some punk kid to emerge with a girl that was assumed dead.

He had jumped for the case, sensing there was more to it in the way that the boy had described things in such vivid detail. It was obviously something close to him and not just a run of the mill psycho weaving stories for mild amusement. King was still surprised at how many nothing cases were derived that way.

Chung however, continued to show him the cold shoulder. He had blown up at King after he had accepted the Evans' case, but then had grudgingly tagged along to keep King company. King suspected he was in it for the glory. If the case were to break, it would be their shot at the big times and they both knew it.

The trap door opened into the centre of an old log cabin. It had been lost in the woods for decades as the foliage swallowed it whole in its abandonment. Only foot trails granted access to the rotting cedar monument that was left alone in the wilderness. The forest had grown thick surrounding it, making it visible only from a few feet away. King and Chung had scoured the area for two hours with their team before the cabin had been found. It had taken them another half an hour to find a way in through the grown over trees and brambles.

Vines had overtaken most of the outer walls giving the place the impression that it was built into the ground itself. They were definitely off the map and the directions the boy had given them had been accurate to the nines. King was getting more and more excited in anticipation of their case. Once they had secured the two into custody it was smooth sailing onto a promotion for him and Chung.

Chung had set up a small generator with a light across from him. The yellow light spilled over the decomposing room seeping into the worn wood. Sheets of dark fabric had been hung around the small room to absorb the light before it escaped into the vast forest, giving away their location. Outside, the backup team sat waiting in the woods.

King didn't feel bad for them outside alone and bored. Six years ago that had been him just starting out, backing up the higher up officers and hoping one day he would get a chance to be the one on the inside.

Chung whipped the last card at the table in a foul mood. "How much longer is this gonna take?" He challenged King with a deserving sneer.

They had been waiting since midday, their boredom growing by the hour.

"I told him twenty four." King reminded him for the sixth time. He was not well known for his patience. Chung snorted, picking the cards up into a pile he began shuffling them lazily, making a show of his boredom as he tapped his foot impatiently against the floor. His foot tapping left a dent in the soft wood as it crumbled upon impact.

"Another round of war?" He suggested "Best of fifty five?"

King nodded. Walking to the pile of wood they were using as a table, he gave one last look over his shoulder at the trap door before sitting. He took the pile of cards and began shuffling; Chung currently held the lead.

***

Hart's entourage continued to speed swiftly to the cabin at the end of the tunnel. After only thirty five minutes they had finally come to the edge of the thick woods that concealed the tunnels exit. The car pulled to the side of the road crossing over thick fresh tire tread and then to a stop.

Hart exited, walking straight into the woods expecting his men to follow. He was not disappointed as they trailed wordlessly behind him. Awaiting his command they fell into position silently scouting the forest surrounding their leader, watching for threats. Hart smiled at their unwavering loyalty and how they instinctively kept him safe.

The brush was overgrown; no path existed to the cabin in the woods. Hart had seen to that fifteen years ago when he had originally purchased the church. He had also purchased the plot of land containing the escape hatch. For it would do Hart no good if the forest was torn down to build another strip mall. He had anticipated the use of the tunnels and strove to keep the exit maintained and hidden from the world. Inquiry into the tunnel beneath the cabin would only lead to speculation about the church. And with a prisoner in the tower, that would have been disastrous for him. He was a cautious man when it came to his captives, leaving no room for error.

The air was fresh and smelled of the damp morning dew that clung fast to the leaves. Hart's three guards walked cautiously and quietly out through the wooded area, making less sound than the wind through the trees. In their dark gear and the light camouflage they had applied while speeding to the cabin, they were nearly undetectable in the lush environment. Even with the autumn leaves splayed across the forest floor, they had managed enough cover within brambles and branches to be undetectable even to the keenest eyes. This was what they had been trained for.

Hart halted several strides into the woods. Raising a hand he indicated that his men scatter. As he stood perfectly still, he listened to his men disarm and drug fifteen hidden agents with little more noise than a tree branch snapping in the distance. Surely they had been outnumbered, but not outsmarted, Hart always held a card up his sleeve.

Within a matter of minutes a whistle ahead sounded like a raven indicating the forest had been cleared of all threats. Hart stepped further in with a practiced precision, careful to keep himself neat while deliberately keeping a rapid pace. He made a straight line to the cabin that he knew was tucked into the woods ahead.

He stepped delicately over a patch of poison oak, following his instincts further into the woods that he had deliberately let grow out into an unruly oasis. Pausing, he admired the simplistic beauty of the trees while his men returned to him. Hart was cautious to check his gun, clicking the safety off before re-holstering it in his belt, facing away from himself as an added measure.

His men stood behind him like statuesque gargoyles ready to lunge forward into an attack. He approached the cabin cautiously, keenly aware that it was occupied. Dim light filtered through the cabin walls, barely visible from their distance. Mild conversations from within indicated that more than one man was inside. Again, Hart halted a few paces away pausing to listen to the noises for a moment, hoping to determine an exact count before sending his small team in.

He lifted his arm and his tiny army shot forward like a bullet aimed at his target. He watched for a moment at the thrill, before turning quietly into the woods. He had other business to attend to at the moment.

***

Chung had taken to pacing like a bad game of pong between the walls of the small cabin while King stood ever vigilant over the trap door. He paused at a noise outside the cabin, turning to King who had also looked up in wonder. Both stood still, listening as noises pressed in from the forest outside. The birds had gone silent. A twig snapped not far off. The silence from the forest was eerie from inside the cabin. They both stood still as statues, eyes glazed over as they concentrated on using their ears, focusing on the forest outside.

The floor groaned as King shifted his weight making them both jump. He shook his head in apology as the two snapped back to the room, leaving the strange noises to the rest of their team to worry about.

In addition to the two agents waiting in the cabin, King had been assigned a detail of fifteen to secure the grounds. It was a preventative measure in the event that the girl was who Ethan had said she was. There hadn't been a high profile case in their district in over fifty years, so the bureau was using this possible rescue mission as training for some of the more rusty agents.

Chung crossed to the back window. It was more of a hole in the cabin wall than anything, a crack between two of the cedar logs. Tilting his head he looked through the opening without moving the sheet they had hung over it. Six men should have been back there under the cover of the thick wooded forest. Chung saw nothing out of the ordinary; it was the same as it had been the last time. Only the snapping of a branch and the rustling of the leaves as the wind circled through the lot, typical forest sounds. They were doing a good job out there with their cover, he would be sure to mention it later to their ranking officer.

Chung stepped back to the centre of the cabin where King was still and silent. He was now crouched cautiously listening to the floorboards, awaiting their guests who were expected to arrive at any moment.

Agent Chung had grown tired of standing still and listening for what was probably an animal in the vast forest. Kneeling down, he shot King a look.

"We done yet?" He whispered, just as the front door was kicked in.

CHARGE

Grace had regained a bit of strength from rehydrating herself. She was famished but no longer woozy and she could tell that Ethan was feeling the same effects from finally having some water.

Looking at the guards for the first time, she noticed how weary they appeared. The night was surely long for them as well and she was well aware that they didn't see much action while guarding the church.

Steve leaned against the damp wall for support sinking in slowly as though it were made of quicksand. He was shaking from the humidity mingling with the chill of the underground and lack of sleep.

Walt had given up standing and had slowly slid down the wall into an awkward half awake pose with his hand at his chin propping his head up above his knees.

Grace looked to Ethan, cautious of the guards noticing them. They communicated with a series of strange looks and nudges. She shifted and slowly lifted her hands to show Ethan her loose ties. She looked at the guards and then shrugged, raising an eyebrow. He nodded, looking more alert himself as adrenaline coursed through his veins in anticipation.

Grace could feel the tie on her hands was looser than it should have been. She guessed that the guards hadn't wanted to hurt their frail prisoner. Grace however, was not frail. She began slowly and carefully twisting her hands out; avoiding the guards' stares as she moved her hands slowly against the tie.

Ethan took notice. He began yawning, and shifting. He tried to take all of the guards' attention over to his side of the tunnel while Grace popped her hands out. Her hands were bloody and raw in the widest parts where she had had to force them through over scrapes from the rough tunnel escape.

Walt stood, Steve left the walls support; both were looking at Ethan and his sudden lack of lethargic movement. Ethan was shifting his legs to support his back against the wall. Slowly he was sliding up the wall into a low standing position. The guards were wary of his movements, both turning their bodies fully to face him.

Leaning in, Grace quietly removed Walt's gun from his holster as he turned. She then snuck unnoticed towards Steve as he commanded Ethan.

"Sit back down, on the ground!"

Grace slipped over to the opposite wall, reaching for Steve's holster. Ethan paused in his struggles, hoping to keep the guards still for a moment. He mocked sickness, breathing slowly and looking to the ground. Arching his back he began to wretch and the guards froze in disgust. Ethan rolled his back and moaned.

Steve stood frozen at his side with his hands up, not willing to reach out and grab someone who was about to be ill. Walt's face was trapped in a look of bewilderment at the sudden illness. He looked concerned that he may have been exposed to the same illness while within the tunnels.

"Stand against the wall." Grace demanded with a loud click as she hit the safety off. Walt and Steve both turned in confusion, horror crossed their faces within a moment. Grace stood with a gun in her hand held at chest height and aimed at Walt's heart. Both guards searched franticly for the second gun keeping their eyes locked on Grace as they patted their belts down. The second gun sat tucked in Grace's waistband.

"I have them both." She stated smugly, saving them the time of their frantic search of the tunnel floor.

Looking up in a state of horror, they backed into the wall simultaneously. Ethan pulled his hands to his face and began chewing through the tie binding them together. Within a few moments, he too was free.

Standing cautiously to avoid blocking Grace's range, Ethan approached Steve from the side and removed the heavy flashlight from his belt. With one last look to Grace, he reached back and hit Steve over the head with a deafening thud. Steve crumpled at the feet of a whimpering Walt. Ethan took a step forward pulling the flashlight up from the ground he repeated the motion, leaving two unconscious guards at his feet.

"Check their bag, it might be helpful." Grace suggested, handing Ethan the gun from her waistband as she knelt down to retrieve the second flashlight.

"No point, the exit is there." He pointed up to a hatch in the ceiling. "I have friends waiting on the other side." He reminded her.

"Finally." She whispered dropping the duffle bag still attached to the guard's back, it landed heavily against the ground spilling its contents through the unzipped main pocket across the floor.

**

Hart's men kicked in the door to the cabin, quickly falling into position as splinters scattered across the floor. The agents met them with two rounds of gunfire, narrowly missing their small triangle of counter-defence.

Tumbling through the door, the men landed in a kneeling position. Firing once each, they leapt to their feet. Fanning out through the room they hoped to catch the agents off guard.

Unabashed, the agents took to the task with a fiery rage that left Hart's men panting, trying to keep up to stay alive. Guns fired, fists flew and the men fought with a ferocity normally reserved for action movie cut-scenes.

King was bleeding. His arm dripped from an early bullet wound. He held one of the intruders with his good arm wrapped around the man's neck. With an abrupt twist, his attacker crumpled to the ground in a silent heap.

King, out of breath, paced to Chung's side where he had been keeping the other two attackers at bay with an array of boxing moves and gun power.

Chung caught King's glance and turned his full attention to the man closest. Flicking the safety on as his hand lifted for a violent uppercut he toppled the man over their makeshift card table. Chung advanced and soon the man was pinned against a wall by his forearm. Chung raised his other arm and knocked the man over the head with his pistol, rendering him unconscious. *Two down, one to go* he thought turning back to King.

***

Ethan heard gunfire overhead.

"Grace stay here." He demanded in a panic as he flipped the hatch open to the chaos above.

Grace ducked away from the light of the opening, instinctively avoiding being seen by the source of the gunfire. She didn't need to be told twice.

Ethan emerged into a mess of broken glass and wood splinters. King held a man to the floor as Chung knocked another out across the room.

Blinking, Ethan's eyes adjusted to the bright light.

King turned towards him.

"Who knew you were coming?" He growled to Ethan.

"Dominic Hart, he sent men after us in the tunnel too."

"He must be here then." King concluded as he knocked out his target and rose to his feet. Walking to the window, he drew back the blinds to

ESCAPE

reveal a stern Hart, standing patiently in the clearing with a look of amusement splayed across his face.

"Shit." King gasped, as he pushed the blinds back into position. "Chung, call in the backup."

Chung pulled a two-way from his belt, twisting a knob he began to mumble into the device. With his back turned to King and Ethan he relayed commands to the outside re-enforcements.

"To command post one, repeat, report to command post one. Over," Chung turned to King, concerned at the lack of response. Finally a static click indicated a response.

"You should expect a delay...as they pull themselves together..."Sounded the thick sarcastic voice of Hart on the other end of the receiver.

Ethan felt his hopes shatter. Even without an entourage, Mr. Hart was a force near unbeatable. He would never let Grace leave. Turning to the hatch, Ethan grasped Grace by the hand helping her through into the disarray of the cabin. She blinked heavily adjusting to the light that had long eluded her. Left with little choice, Ethan turned to King and Chung, waiting for their brilliant plan.

"You got a gun kid?" King asked turning to Ethan as he checked the rounds in his own pistol splayed open in his hands.

"Yes, two if you count the one Grace has."

"Let her keep hers." He continued, taken off guard by the good luck "We go out the front, a triad surrounding the girl."

"Hart won't make a move if he's alone." Chung agreed hoping that their profiler was right about him, they were taking a big risk.

The three men positioned themselves around Grace. Ethan and Chung took flank, each maintaining a point of contact at Grace's elbow while King stood in the front. Grace stayed close behind his back, knowing that they were avoiding something on the other side of the door.

King kicked the door outwards. It flew off of its hinges as the last of the rotting wood gave way. They raced through the opening, straight towards Hart, who stood waiting with leaves whirling around his stiff figure.

Grace looked up into Hart's eyes with shock, "Father?"

HART

Grace went stiff as her eyes met her fathers. She had not seen him since her last escape attempt four years ago. The agents brushed her past him with little more than one last snide remark from the stoic criminal.

"No one escapes, my dear Gracie." He smirked as they slid past into the vast forest. Trekking through the thick brush, Chung faced backwards staying a few paces behind. He anticipated retaliation from Hart.

King was deep in a whispered conversation on his Bluetooth. Grace could hear his voice strain with frustration. He clicked at his ear a moment later and wheeled around to face Ethan.

"You could have told us Hart was her father." He scowled at Ethan, "You almost cost us our lives." He looked wildly to Grace taking her in with a curiosity that was normally reserved for animals at the zoo. "We are getting out of here." He noted, quietly as Chung caught up.

They continued silently through the trees for a few moments longer before the trees began thinning out and they came out at a small clearing.

A black car sat tucked under a sparse netted covering. It remained hidden from sight until King had pulled back on the ropes, dispersing a thin layer of autumn foliage across the ground as he shook the mesh off of the vehicle.

Chung took point, standing with Grace and Ethan while King inspected their car for signs of ambush. King made several laps of the car before allowing Grace and Ethan into the back seats. Grace crawled in, grateful for the soft seats and the blanket that King tossed over his shoulder to her. With a click, King turned the car on, cranking the heat to warm Grace and Ethan after their underground adventure.

Grace lifted her head. The air smelled familiar, her eyes grew large with shock as she recognized the scent. Covering her mouth to the putrid stench of chloroform blasting in through the vents with the blanket, she climbed forward. She tugged at Chung's jacket, pulling a radio and phone from his pocket as he collapsed forward onto the dashboard. Reaching over Kings firm grip on the steering wheel, she clicked the keys out of the ignition allowing the vents to grow still.

It was already too late, she was woozy. Stuffing the items into her shirt, Grace wrapped the blanket tightly around herself to keep them in place. She slowly rolled the manual window down just a crack to air the car out. Using the last of her energy she lay onto the back seat, fighting to stay conscious while looking just as unconscious as everyone else in the car. She would have to play possum.

The dizziness had lifted within a few moments and although no one else was stirring Grace could hear a voice. It sounded far away and was growing closer. It was like listening to one side of a conversation. As it grew close enough to be outside her door, she realized it was Hart. With a click she could feel the breeze tumbling in through the now open door. She continued to feint unconsciousness, clutching at the phone and the radio under the blanket.

"Grace my dear." Her father whispered through the door, slyly, "Time to come home."

She cringed at the thought of going back to the tower, or more likely

ESCAPE

the next secret hideaway he had in line for her. Still, she remained quiet. She felt a tug as her father pulled her from the car and slung her over his shoulder. He began walking from the car, stopping after a dozen paces where he set her to the ground.

She could hear the leaves crunching back towards the car. Then he was pouring, something with a sloshing down the back of the car. She could hear it dripping back onto the wet leaves. She opened her eyes enough to peek over.

He was pouring from a red gas can, filling every inch of the car with gasoline. Grace knew her father and his obsession with fire. He used it to clean up almost every crime scene he created. She let out a gasp as she put it all together.

She quickly realized that the noise had blown her cover. She hopped to her feet and scampered off farther into the woods, hoping to distract her father long enough to save Ethan from the tremendous blaze that was intended to kill him and his companions.

She could hear her father giving chase into the woods, making it clear that she was more important captured than they were dead, at least for now. Grace ducked and ran through brambles and bushes. The thick carpet of leaves on the forest floor gave her traction on her bare wet feet. The air was so fresh and rejuvenating; at times she lost herself in the enjoyment of the forest and forgot the chase. Grace continued running faster.

Pulling the cell phone from her shirt she fumbled with it while darting though the trees. Grace had never had a cell phone. Her father had let her use his a couple of times when she was a kid. Things had changed greatly since then. It took her three hills to figure out how to unlock the screen. Then when it began asking for a password, a frustrated Grace gave up.

Tucking it back into her shirt she grabbed out the radio, clicking it on, it was much easier for her to figure out.

"KING!" She yelled into the receiver. Running faster, she changed course, knowing her father would hear her. She had looped back around to the cabin. Hiding with her back against the building in a shrubbery, she could see if her father was approaching now.

She would wait it out until King and his partner got back to her. They should be waking by now. She prayed that Hart hadn't returned to the car to set it on fire just yet.

He probably assumed they had woken anyway and was settling for a second round of his psychotic death match sometime in the near future, he would need to catch Grace first.

Grace could hear a car horn through the woods. She breathed in relief, knowing they were safe for a while.

***

King woke up with his face plastered against the wheel. He shifted as the grogginess washed away, landing his cheek right against the horn. He jumped at the noise while he blinked away his tiredness. He looked in confusion to Chung, who sat beside him searching his coat like something vital was missing.

"What happened?" Ethan yawned from the backseat, barely registering where he was in the haze. With a sudden jump he began looking frantically around, "Where is Grace?" He gasped, pulling on King's collar in a panic, turning the agent to see the empty spot in the back seat where Grace had once been.

King shook Ethan lose of his shirt and turned to the back to check for the girl. The seat was empty and the blanket he had tossed to her was also gone. The car hadn't moved it was still parked in the woods near the cabin. King stepped out of the car stumbling as his head cleared.

"Hart... Hart was here." He frowned, looking the car over. He leaned forward sniffing at the car interior.

Ethan exited the car with Chung on the other side, looking at each other and then to King as though he was losing it.

"The car is covered in gasoline. Get back." King finally spoke in a firm voice as he backed away from the car.

He was unsure of how the explosion was going to be triggered, only that the car was set to go up in flames any moment. Chung and Ethan followed him away from the car and towards the cabin that they had come from. "The SWAT team parked on the other side, we'll take their van." He mumbled to a confused Ethan. "Hart killed them before you and Grace got out of the tunnel."

Ethan stared through the immense forest. He felt like a lead weight had lowered itself into his stomach. The chloroform was still wearing off and he was foggy as to what was actually happening. He stumbled on tree roots, staggering after King and Chung as though he was drunk. He fell; a tree caught him at the last moment before he hit the ground. He blinked heavily, looking forward to the others. He was spinning in his head as he fumbled though the trees at a faster pace than he thought he could ever muster.

King stopped short watching in an agitated manner as his partner tore at his coat pockets in search of something.

"You're missing what?" King spun shakily to Chung, "your phone..." A strange look passed over King's tired face. For a moment he looked like an evil professor.

"Yeah, I can't find it. It was on me when we got in the car, this pocket here." Chung pointed to his chest pocket, "Gone, and it was new." He sulked imitating a phone vanishing into thin air. He continued to search his pocket for a moment longer.

"Well let's call it, get tech to trace the call." King seemed enthusiastic. Reaching into his pocket and producing his own phone, he fumbled with the screen as he held it to his ear. He dialed, looking back to the car half expecting Chung's phone to be a trigger.

It began to ring.

***

Grace could hear noises rustling in the brush ahead of her. She shrunk further into the shrubbery, making herself invisible. Pulling out the phone again, she fumbled past the lock screen into the password screen again.

Where are the buttons? She thought with frustration. Turning the thing over again and again, the screen had gone dark. Grace was just about to give up on it when it began vibrating in her hand, the screen lit up on its own.

It read "King" and showed a picture of one of Ethan's friends from the cabin. She fumbled to unlock the phone, putting it against her ear. She tentatively spoke, "Hello?"

"Grace?" The voice on the other end was King. He sounded far away and slightly dazed.

"Yes it's me. I'm behind the cabin." Grace whispered into the phone, holding it away from her ear so she could listen to the forest for Hart. He could be anywhere near her hiding spot, waiting her out.

She kept the phone away from her ear, listening as a rustling grew closer. She peeked cautiously past her shrubbery and caught the tail of a rabbit hopping ahead into a bush. Relieved, she brought the phone back to her ear.

The call had been terminated. Grace fumbled, tucking it back into her shirt. She sat back against the side of the cabin. The rough wood tickled at her neck, crumbling from years of decay. She felt the wall with her hand; it was soft like sand, tingling as it fell apart under her touch. As she watched, she could see birds fluttering from tree to tree. The forest was so alive. She watched with wonder as a chipmunk skittered up a tree to her right with a mouth full of food.

She looked curiously at the moss creeping up the trees around her. It was all on the same side, like the compass direction affected its growth. It had been so long since she had sat in a forest and back then she surely didn't appreciate the delicate intricacy of nature surrounding her. Flies buzzed by, loud as they passed her head. She could see insects trailing down the brush of the shrubbery she hid in.

When she was younger the bugs might have frightened her. Now she was glad to see them, glad that not everything in the world had changed while she was gone. Grace was hoping that King had heard her and was on his way. She would give him thirty minutes, then she was getting out of there on her own. She began to count to herself in a hushed whisper, "One...two...three..."

Her eyes were growing heavy. The adrenaline that had seeped through her during her escape was slipping away. Grace was having trouble focusing on the numbers, instead she found herself mutely watching the trees swaying calmly in the gentle autumn breeze. The sight was hypnotizing, gently rocking her to sleep. She could feel her back sliding down the wood of the cabin as she drifted to sleep, fighting less and less to keep her eyes open. She fell asleep listening to the crinkling leaves falling in the breeze.

GUARDED

King had tucked his phone back into the breast pocket of his black suit. He turned to face Chung and Ethan as though they had missed the short conversation in the otherwise quiet forest.

"She's at the cabin." He whispered, looking through the forest for signs of movement, aware that Hart was still lurking somewhere in its vastness.

Ethan looked back at the empty forest, unsure from which way they had come, let alone where the cabin might be hidden. He was lost in the colourful greens and earthly oranges and browns that surrounded him. If King and Chung were to slip behind a tree he feared he would be lost forever. He completed his turn. Facing back towards King, who was pulling his phone back out.

"Glad we marked that place in the GPS." He mumbled to Chung as he fiddled with the touch screen in his dirty hands. King looked up, holding the phone flat against his open palm. He pointed to Ethan, looking past him into the thick trees. "That way." He mumbled, looking back down to his hand as he stepped forward.

Ethan let him pass and fell in behind Chung. He kept up, hoping that he wouldn't get lost in the endless woods. They intimidated him after the confines of the tunnels. Slick moss squished under his feet. Broken trees gave way on the forest floor as they were stepped on, collapsing into small plumes of pollen. Ethan sneezed, running to catch up.

King was making good time. He had nearly walked into several trees before being pulled to the side at the last second by Chung. At this pace they would be there in moments. The cabin was still not visible from their vantage point. King looked up expecting to see it but instead he was met by a wall of trees and bushes. Somewhere in the thick of it sat the cabin. And somewhere nearby was Grace.

"Grace?" Ethan called out in a hushed voice. He waited, expecting a rustle somewhere in the brush, indicating where she was hidden. Nothing happened.

"Well, start looking. Look for signs that she may have *left* too." Chung took charge, walking to the other side of the small building.

Ethan walked closer until her could see the outside walls faintly through the brush and brambles that had taken it over. He peered through the bush towards the ground, poking leaves out of his way hoping to see Grace's golden orange hair tangled in the branches below.

So far he was having no luck. He stooped down lower to see better into the undergrowth. Sneezing, his hand slipped toppling him over. He felt something soft brushing against his palm.

Ethan shifted to get a better look. A pair of cold glazed eyes stared back at him. He was dressed in camouflage and crumpled into the earth.

It was one of Kings SWAT team. The position of his neck and the composure of his body sent Ethan reeling back, scrambling away from the dead man. He covered his mouth to stifle the shocked gasp that had escaped him echoing deep into the woods.

King came running up beside him. He could feel his face going white with shock. He pointed to the bush, "Your, your..." King stepped closer to investigate.

"Shit." Ethan heard him mutter under his breath. King backed away from the bushes taking Ethan by the hand and helping him up. "Go to the other side, I'll keep looking here." He gave Ethan a shove to the left, sending him around the corner to look through the foliage.

Ethan paused once around the corner, catching his breath. He was afraid he had made too much noise in his shock of finding the body. He feared Hart would find them. Ethan jumped into his search with a vengeful hatred of Hart propelling him to search faster and faster. He overturned branches and debris, hoping to find Grace lodged somewhere in the tangle at the base of the cabin. Instead he found more moss, weeds, and dirt.

His fingers were filthier now than they had been in the underground labyrinth of the tunnels. He wiped the sweat off of his forehead, smearing a splotch of moss across his face as he did. She had to be there. She wouldn't have moved and they surely would have heard if Hart had found her and tried to drag her off. She would have put up a fight.

Finally after a third patch of prickly brambles had scraped at Ethan's arms, he heard Chung whistle from the opposite side of the shanty chalet. Ethan dusted his hands off as best as he could on his mud crusted pant legs, and climbed through the brush to reach Chung. He was stooped low, heaving something from under a large shrubbery. Orange tangles caught in the branches, Ethan stepped forward to help keep her hair from tangling further while Chung lifted her out.

Grace was drowsy she was blinking slowly as though she had just woken up. Chung tipped her gently into a standing position, letting her feet touch-down slowly while being cautious of her still-bare footing. She clung to him for a moment longer, regaining her balance while swaying slightly from side to side. She let his arm go finally as she looked at Ethan groggily, wary of his reaction.

"It was Hart…" She trailed off, catching herself on Ethan's arm as he stepped closer. She whispered. "He used chloroform in the vents"

King had finally joined them. Covered in blood and dirt, he stayed back quietly wiping his hand before fumbling with his phone again.

There." He stated gruffly, walking towards the tree he had pointed towards. Ethan and Chung followed, supporting a lethargic Grace between them as they stumbled back through the dense trees towards the SWAT van that waited on the other side of the woods.

The trail to the van seemed longer than Ethan had expected. He was sure King was walking in circles, but in the mood he was in no one was brave enough to confront him. He would stop and glare back for them to do the same and then stand still as a statue for a moment or two listening to the trees. With a quick look at his palm he would start up again, not waiting for them to follow.

The droning sound of their feet trudging through the trees was taking up a rhythm in Ethan's head. He felt like the little engine that could, climbing further and further. Just as he was about to speak, to hear any other sound, they popped out of the trees into a clearing with a rarely used dirt road.

Ethan stood looking for a van, while King scoured the site with a little more enthusiasm. He pulled a wet looking set of keys from his belt and pushed a button. A horn sounded behind them, startling them after the quiet of the woods. Ethan nearly dropped Grace in the surprise of it all.

King pounced at the noise, lunging into a cover of leaves and shrubs. He tugged at them like a lunatic, unveiling piece by piece, a covered black SWAT van. Opening the driver's side door he slid across to start the ignition, and then quickly backed away leaving the door open.

"Give it a few minutes, just in case." He mumbled to Chung, obviously trying to make up for his earlier mistake by not making it a second time.

They sat in the woods on a pile of leaves waiting while the engine warmed up. Far enough away that if anything did go wrong, they would still be safe.

Grace and Ethan lay back on the unfolded blanket looking to the upper foliage. Grace counted the leaves as they plunged from the trees, swiftly soaring in arcs and loops through the sky.

Ethan watched her quietly taking in the differences in her face over the years away from him. She smiled at a leaf that brushed past her cheek, and Ethan smiled too, glad that her smile hadn't changed on him too.

***

Hart had exhausted his time, Grace had escaped. How she had resisted the lull of the chloroform he was unsure. Knowing the agents and that putrid boy would be stirring soon, left him no choice but to leave post haste. He had no backup and they were well trained.

He had weighed his options and decided that he would take another approach. Hart walked a straight line with a sense of dignity about him. His suit was soiled from patches of wet in the forest's higher undergrowth. He held his head high, moving with a sense of purpose. He marched straight through the greens and burnt oranges onto the patch of wet gravel he had parked in earlier.

He bowed down at the side of the car. Tucking his hand under the passenger wheel well he felt around briefly, locating a hide-a-key tucked away beneath. He pulled it out and sliding it open, he discarded the case after retrieving the key.

Hart circled to the driver side, disregarding the traffic swerving in the lanes beside him. He clicked the door opened, and slid in. Starting the engine he revved forward with a backwards glance to the forest beside him. He would return later to finish up some business there. For now he moved on to more important matters.

ESCAPE

***

Grace stared at the branches weaving together above her. She pretended that beyond them were stars. Later at night, the forest would be beautiful she thought to herself smiling. She couldn't help herself but to smile at every little thing out back in the real world.

Even if her father were to capture her again, she had made enough happy memories already to get her through to her next escape attempt. She still hoped that it wouldn't come to that. She watched overhead as leaves plunged towards her, wiggling free of their secure holdings on their branches. She felt like a leaf floating away from captivity herself. She relished in the release of the spiralling leaf above her, smiling at its floating dance towards the ground. If only her own escape could be so poetic and graceful.

King stood, staying still for a moment before walking to the van. He inspected it again, trailing through every detail. Turning the engine off again, he lifted the hood to inspect each part. He crawled along the sides on his hands and knees peering under at the undercarriage. Finally he determined that it was safe enough for them to enter.

Chung leapt at him, prying the keys from his hand. "Passenger side." Chung muttered to him, loud enough for Grace to hear over the crinkling leaves.

Grace and Ethan stood shaking the blanket out before entering the back of the spacious van. The trunk alone was nearly as big as her tower confines, and so much cleaner. She couldn't help but smile again.

Grace crawled across to the padded bench in the back, sprawling lazily across nearly the entire thing. Ethan took up his post at her head, piling a lumpy first aid kit under her head like a pillow. She was asleep almost immediately. He tucked the damp blanket that she had dragged through the brush with her over her shaking shoulders.

She was convulsing in her sleep from the cold and he worried how sick she may have gotten. The van pulled forward with a gentle rocking motion that soon had Ethan fighting to keep his eyes open himself.

Ethan and Grace slept while Chung drove to a motel. King was on his phone calling ahead for backup and reporting the cabin massacre of their last team.

The road wound out of the thick forest and into a small town. The air was damp with an impending storm as they pulled into a motel.

The building was decrepit. Something surely beneath the use of the FBI, which was exactly why Chung had chosen it. It was far enough off the radar that it would be hard for Hart to track them in.

The motel was two levels, a long narrow building that coiled back unevenly along a cracking pavement parking lot. Chung hopped down from the driver's seat, dodging into the front lobby. He left the car running with King glancing anxiously across the plot, leaning to see around other parked cars suspiciously.

Soon Chung returned with a key. He pointed to King. They had a room up the stairs on the second floor. It would be hard to gain access to, save for a rickety set of stairs that would likely give an intruder away before they could reach the door. King nodded with approval, dialing his phone to notify the tech team on the other end.

"Team two arrives in twenty. Let's order these kids some food." Chung suggested as he lifted Grace gingerly from the back of the van. Ethan rose groggily, awake enough to make it up the steps and in the door before falling asleep again in a chair awkwardly. Chung placed Grace on the bed, covering her up with the fresh white bed linens while they waited.

King nodded, reaching again for his phone as he locked the door and drew the curtains closed.

BLUFF

Mr. Hart remained calm. Plucking his cell from the breast pocket of his neat suit, he pressed one number and held it. Bringing the phone to his ear, he whispered, "Phase two." and hung up.

That boy had looked too familiar, like a business partner he had grudgingly put down years ago. Hart presumed that filthy child was the same one that had penetrated his church by leaping over the wall and stirred this mess up. The others were obviously federal agents. This would require an amount of finesse to cover up that Hart had not had to exact in years.

Not since he had kidnapped his own daughter and faked her death. As a breeze whistled through the open window, he frowned. He was going to miss the football game tonight.

Hart reached into the back seat, producing a duffle bag. He tugged it over onto the passenger seat and began to rifle through it while he sped down the interstate. Plucking out a stick of explosives, he smiled, knowing that if he did it just right he could claim the insurance money for the accident.

He pulled into the church lot, whipping across the lawn before screeching to a skittering halt outside the main doors. Hart exited the car, duffle bag in tow. He looked the great facade of the old church over one more time before entering. The worn wooden doors swung in the breeze, no longer locked in place by the pegs in the floor. He made his way to the basement to set his equipment up making quick time. He would soon have to turn around and take care of the cabin as well.

Hart ducked into the farthest corners of the cellar, crawling professionally over the rubble of previous excavations. He tethered sticks to each corner and lastly to the beam that supported the entrance to the tunnels.

Hart would have been happier taking the whole tunnel system out with the church, but would settle for this sacrifice. As he wound the coil back out the front door he glanced down at a twinkling in the nearby brush. He walked over cautiously, uncoiling the detonator as he walked.

A leather briefcase sat in the bushes outside of the church doors, *Evans* was scrawled across a brass nameplate stamped across the top. Fire welled up in Harts eyes. He paused to look down at the case. *Evans* he thought; *then I suppose it is him*. Hart smiled smugly taking the briefcase with him as he rolled his way back into the car.

Hart pressed his foot to the floor, key still in the ignition. He wound the cord past the rock walls surrounding the building. Fury was rising in Hart's throat. Grace would not elude him. He knew her like his own daughter, perhaps because she was.

With a flick of a switch, the church was set ablaze.

***

Ethan awoke to the smell of warm pizza and the sound of Chung closing the door. Light filtered slowly away as the click of the door shut it out.

Rubbing the kinks out of his neck he rolled forward out of the lumpy dirty chair he had been folded into. The room was dark, with the curtains drawn closed. Only the glow of the bathroom was casting shadows across the small room. Ethan walked to the cramped dining area where three boxes of pizza now sat piled teetering on a small metal table.

King sat at the table in a small creaking chair. He looked up to Ethan from his slice of pepperoni pizza. His face was cold in the faint light; he appeared pensive with a furrowed brow.

"You forgot to tell us Grace was Mr. Hart's *daughter*, Ethan." Kings eyes shot daggers from across the table as he reminded Ethan of the facts that had been left out of his original report. "Good men were killed out there." He snorted. His arm twitched as he set his slice down on the table. He looked about ready to pounce. He sat poised waiting for Ethan to respond.

Ethan reached for a slice, looking to the floor ashamed.

Quickly swallowing a bite of pizza Ethan looked to Chung for support. "I didn't think you would believe me." He replied.

"Believe you?" Yelled King, "Why on Earth would he lock his own daughter up!" He stood from the table, scraping his chair across the floor already grooved with marks from the rickety metal chair. "Of course I wouldn't have believed you; I watched her funeral ten years ago! It was pretty public." King was pacing now, shaking his head as though he had rehearsed these lines over and over on their trip to the motel. He looked straight at Ethan, stopping inches from his face. "You could have given us some proof, Ethan. Isn't the story that she was killed with your own father?"

King was outraged; he had been led blindly into a trap by an idiot. He was accountable for all the men that had died at the cabin. He would be lucky if the relief team didn't relieve him of his duties. He could see the hurt look on Ethan's face and wondered briefly if he had gone too far, dragging the kid's dad into it. It was such a mess and Chung looked smug standing in the corner with his arms lazily crossed. King had never been so furious.

"No." Squeaked Ethan after a moment. He backed away from King's face. "Hart killed my father and used it as a cover-up to hide Grace. She was a liability or something." He trudged on, looking to the sleeping Grace for comfort. "I think she has information that could end him. So he hid her away." Ethan looked to King, "She has enough evidence to put Hart behind bars... somewhere." He concluded, reaching for a second slice of pizza as his stomach turned in knots.

He fell loudly into a second aluminum chair, scraping beneath him as it slid slowly under his weight on the uneven floor. Ethan hoped his indiscretion would not cause his rescue to fail. He could not bear losing Grace to her evil father again and the repercussions would surely ensure his own death. He shook with fear, covering it up by biting into the slice of pizza shaking in his hand.

Grace began to stir. The room fell silent in anticipation. They all looked to one another hoping she hadn't overheard their conversation, looking guilty and trying to cover it up by reaching for more pizza.

Sitting up groggily Grace took in the room, blinking as her eyes adjusted to the harsh dimness of the place. "Is that real pizza?" She asked Ethan bemused.

She squinted as she looked to the tiny alcove of a kitchen. She smiled as the smell reached her, breathing in heavily the aromatic scent of pizza. She struggled to get her legs free of the confines of the bed linens.

Standing, Ethan crossed the room, placing a half empty box of pepperoni and cheese at the end of the bed for Grace.

Greedily she swiped a slice and began eating. "Mmmmmm..." She garbled through a mouthful of pizza. She smiled through her chewing, blissfully enjoying her first taste of real food in such a long while.

The others stopped to watch her for a moment, almost forgetting how long she had been out of the real world until that moment. Thinking of the little things that they took for granted, and there Grace was, trapped in the confines of her father's rage for ten years of her short life, sitting and enjoying a fresh slice of pizza. Ethan smiled at her exuberant joy.

"Grace..." King began, reluctant to interrupt her in her pizza haven. She was already on her third slice.

A banging at the door interrupted him. She looked up mid-bite with curiosity.

Rising from his chair, he crossed the room to the door slowly. Checking the peephole first, he opened the door with a relieved sigh.

"It's about time, this is a raging mess. Tell me you brought enough backup." He peeked into the parking lot searching.

A tall stern man appeared in the door. "Agent, we are removing the girl from your custody for transfer to a safe house. You are to report to base for debriefing."

The man pushed past King towards Grace with an air of arrogance. As the light from outside filtered into the room Grace could tell she didn't trust that man.

His hair was sleeked back and his face appeared to be stuck in a menacing sneer. He looked over the room, and then Grace. He stopped at the foot of the bed, looking intently at a tousled Grace, waiting impatiently while tapping his large foot.

She looked up over her slice of pizza, defiantly biting down. Chewing, she waited for a reaction from him. He scowled, turning away from her. He held out his hand, waiting for Grace to stand and follow him.

"I'm going with her." Ethan demanded. He stopped a foot away and a foot shorter than the new agent.

"I'm sorry son, you are not authorized to travel with her." The man turned to Ethan with a look of disgust, "Perhaps it would be best for you to go have a shower." He said with a scowl.

"Can agent Chung come with me?" Grace interrupted, not fully trusting the new agent and his intimidating demeanor.

She looked to Chung for support. He jumped forward, seeing the look of pleading in Grace's eyes. He could tell she was uncomfortable around the new agent. He couldn't quite shake the feeling that something wasn't quite right about the sneering giant himself.

"Yes." Chung agreed, interrupting before the man could speak. "I will stay with her."

The new agent raised a brow, looking to Chung as though sizing him up. "Then it is settled." He concluded, "We leave immediately."

Plucking Grace up by an elbow he gently pulled her to the door. Chung followed her out, wrapping his jacket around her tiny shoulders for warmth.

Grace looked back over her shoulder to Ethan and King, both standing confused in the quiet motel room. "Thank you." She whispered over her shoulder as she was tugged out of sight.

Ethan fell to the end of the bed, bouncing on the lumpy mattress as he sunk into oblivion. He stared after Grace watching as the last trace of her orange hair whisked away out of sight. He looked to the far wall of the room, willing his eyes not to water up. He hoped that was not the end of his friendship with Grace, but he couldn't help feeling like she was being ripped away all over again.

King stood seething at the open door. With one last shake of his head he threw the door closed with a resounding bang and walked back to the table of pizza boxes.

***

At the foot of the steps a black car sat idling. The windows were tinted enough to give Chung trouble looking in. He could see a driver still sitting behind the wheel.

"You are up front with Smybert." The agent nodded to Chung. Stepping back as the door swung open, "I will sit with the girl in back."

He tugged Grace's arm once more, propelling her away from the back door as he swung it open, narrowly missing agent Chung as he entered the front seat.

The doors clicked closed as the engine purred. Chung looked the car over. It didn't look like the standard issue. The ID number was missing from the dash and the seats were stained from several coffees that had spilled out of the broken cup holder between the passenger and driver seats.

Chung looked out the window. The tint was streaked from this side and looked cheaply done. He reached into his pocket and slipped out his cellular phone that he had retrieved from Grace in the woods. He tucked it into the back of the seat as he fumbled with his belt. If anything went wrong at least they would be able to track the vehicle.

More often than not, he would end up spending twenty minutes fishing his phone back out of mistreated company cars that only looked sketchy, but you could never be too sure in his line of work.

Grace was relieved as she settled into the scratchy leather seat. At least at a safe-house Hart wouldn't be able to find her. She wished Ethan had been allowed to come along too. She hoped that she could talk them in to keeping him safe from her father.

She frowned, sitting in the back seat next to the tall slimy looking man. Something about him was oddly familiar.

"This won't take long." He assured Chung from his spot in the backseat.

They settled in and the car began at a screeching pace. Peeling out from the lot it sent up a plume of dirt and rock. Chung looked back confused. Just in time to see the agent beside Grace raise his pistol and slam it back into Chung's temple.

Grace looked to the driver in horror.

These were not friends of Ethan.

This was not a backup team; this was Harts last ditch attempt to get her back in the tower. Her mouth screamed silently agape at the horror. She had been through this enough to know they would be nicer if she were quiet. She looked frantically for an escape route. The car was going too fast to get out the door. She kept looking.

PURSUIT

Ethan washed himself up in the restroom while King checked over and packed his last few items with a slice of pizza hanging from his chin.

"You want a ride kid?" King asked from the other room over a mouth full of food. "You should come in with me, they might have questions."

"Yeah, okay."

Ethan turned off the restroom light and stepped back into the room. King was standing in the door, talking to someone. He turned to Ethan stiffly.

"We have a problem kid..."

Ethan raced to the door. Standing outside were two neatly dressed agents, below them several dark vans sat idling.

"*This* was our backup." King concluded as he raced out the door speaking rapidly with the new agents.

Ethan followed close behind, catching only snippets of the conversation. He could tell by their tone that there had been a serious miscalculation. Heads were going to roll.

Ethan was in a panic. Who had just taken Grace and Chung from the motel? Didn't these men have some sort of protocol, a secret password or something to stop things like this from happening?

He was in shock when King tugged at his arm, leading him down the rusted stairs. Thunder boomed and with a crackle in the distance, rain began to fall in sheets soaking Ethan as he raced along behind King trying to hear what he was saying to the other man.

A sleek black car sat at the front of the swat team cavalcade. The two agents slid inside. King opened the back passenger door, waving his hand for Ethan to climb in first.

Ethan ducked out of the rain and slid across the soft leather seat to the driver side, looking to King for information. Even a look on his face to tell him what was going on.

"They were heading North." King reminded the driver, shaking his hair out into the back seat like a wet dog as he closed the door beside him. The car sped forward, leaving Ethan searching for a seatbelt to hold on to. The convoy followed with flashing lights.

***

Grace was panicking, were they taking her back to her father, or the tower? Maybe they already had a new tower lined up for her. Ethan would never find her. The man beside her reached over forcefully, clutching her hands together in her lap. Outside it had started pouring. Grace couldn't see out the window the rain was coming too fast. The car slowed down as he gripped her hands tighter.

"Sit tight, this will be over soon." He sneered putting a damp cloth to her mouth.

Instinctively she held her breath. The chloroform had been used on her too many times before. She faked fainting again, and slightly dizzy she held on to her consciousness. She felt hands on her, folding her into the space at the foot of the seat, a blanket being tossed over her. No one would see her now. Hearing movement she knew the man was climbing up front.

An opening door and a grunt indicated Chung had been expelled from the vehicle. The door clicked and the car sped up. The wipers sloshed quickly across the front window. Grace held her hand over her mouth to hold in the gasp that threatened to escape her lips.

"How long to the cut off Doug." Said the man from the backseat, breaking the monotone ticking of the rain against the roof.

"Half an hour, but there's a truck stop in five, could stop for a bite while she's out?" Doug suggested.

"Exactly." His companion chuckled as the car sped on.

The blanket covering Grace was itchy and made her nose twitch. She felt like she was going to sneeze. She counted in her head to ten trying to stifle off the urge without moving under the blanket. The routine was familiar to her.

She would wait until they had exited the car and then continue her search for a safe escape route. She hoped they hadn't been clever enough to click on the child locks back there. It always made it harder to escape if you had to crawl over into the front seat to do it.

Five minutes later Grace felt the car pull off onto a gravel drive. It dipped, splashing in the quick filling puddles. Swerving to the left, the car parked and the doors clicked as the men exited. Their footsteps rapidly splashed in the puddles outside.

She could faintly hear the ding of the diner door as it opened. Light music wafted out with the smells of homemade fries and burgers. Grace peeked from under the blanket, adjusting herself to see the diner out the window. She waited. Dark dripping rainclouds provided her cover from wandering eyes, as drips of water trailed down the windows.

Grace crouched patiently for a few minutes before she felt sure enough to slip out the door and creep behind the car. Taking in her surroundings she searched for the fastest escape route that would provide cover if anyone looked out the window. *Maybe cover from the rain too*, she thought. Her light clothing had already soaked through under agent Chung's heavy coat. She slipped behind the next car, standing in the middle of a deep puddle for a pause. Then she made a dash for a patch of trees adjacent to the lot of cars.

***

The new agents flew down the interstate. Weaving through traffic at dangerous speeds they sent up a mist of rain behind them. They knew Hart's men had a twenty minute lead and were trying to close the gap as quickly as possible.

Peters, the driver, was hunched over and gripping the wheel. He appeared like a kid trying to win a racing game. He smiled slightly every time he narrowly dodged an accident or produced a horn from a passing car. His partner, Platt, sat stiffly scowling while he waited for their in-house tech team to identify the car.

King stared out the side window lost in thought. Their damp clothing gave the car a stifling smell. Platt had turned the heaters on high to warm them up as they dried off. It hissed at Ethan's ear as he leaned against the back headrest trying to scavenge together enough of a plan to get Grace back again.

He hoped they could find her, or at least the car. He was willing to go undercover as one of Hart's men to get her out, but Hart looked as though he had recognized him when they had walked past him at the cabin. Ethan's head was swimming with ideas and excuses. He needed to see that Grace was found safe and he knew that he was willing to do just about anything to make sure of it...facing Hart was another story.

Ethan wasn't sure if he could count on the new agents to help him with his cause. Surely he could use some of their resources if he kept them close enough, but he wouldn't trust them with Grace's life again. Not after all of their blunders with her rescue.

Ethan sat up and looked from one agent to another, searching for their hidden agenda. He hoped that he could read in their faces if they had ulterior motives or were really in this to save Grace. King, who was staring lazily out the back window sat up straight and yelled at Peters.

"Pull over."

Peters looked in the rear view mirror amused, "What for?" He asked.

"That was Chung at the side of the road, I'm sure of it." King declared sternly.

Peters didn't wait for more information. The car jerked as it decelerated onto the shoulder sending a wash of mud spraying across the roads shoulder and then again as it began moving backwards. Peters' face turned to look out the back window as he reversed. The car abruptly stopped.

King's door flew open.

Turning to look out the back window, Ethan saw King stoop by an unconscious Chung. He lay bleeding at the side of the road, soaked and covered in mud. Trails of water washed away from him like tiny dark rivers carrying his blood away off the side of the road into the thick forest. Ethan imagined the animals lurking on the other side of the wall of trees, drawn to the smell of blood like wolves and shuttered.

Tracks leading towards Chung indicated the impact he had had with the wet muck as he hit the ground from a moving vehicle. Platt stepped out to give King a hand. Delicately they carried him to the car, placing his head on Ethan's lap.

King climbed back in to the now crowded and muddy back seat. He began looking over Chung's wounds, checking his pulse and wiping muck from his wounds by ringing water from the sleeve of his dripping coat.

Platt passed him a small first aid kit from the glove compartment. The vehicle smelled of dampness and blood, Ethan was reminded of the tunnel.

He gritted his teeth as Chung lay unconscious in his lap.

"We good here?" Peters asked.

King nodded, opening the first aid. The car sped forward, hydroplaning before winding back into traffic.

FLIGHT

Grace darted for the tree line after one glance back at the diner. Rain pelted her face. She slipped into a deep puddle before making it across the lot. Once under the cover of trees, bushes and roadside debris she felt safe. She peeked back to be sure her fumble hadn't caught any attention.

When she was sure that she was safe, she smiled and turned into the trees. She decided to continue on, as far from the diner as possible. Once they knew she was gone, they were sure to follow. She didn't want to be within their range. Luckily she knew her father's tracking dogs would be useless after this nasty storm. Any trace of her trail through the woods would be long gone before the night fell. Lightning struck close by as she ducked further into the trees, pulling Chung's jacket tightly around her. The rumble was not long after.

Grace put the diner squarely behind her. Looking forward into the dripping trees, she took off. Jumping over logs, old tires and car parts, Grace found herself full of energy. The fresh air smelled slightly of gasoline, wet earth and metal but after ten years of stale air the thrill was overwhelming. Grace waded through a small creek filled with sharp rocks and broken glass, her feet throbbed as they bled.

The further she got from the diner, the less debris cluttered the ground, making it softer on her tired bare feet. Keeping a good pace she continued uphill pausing at the top to listen for potential followers. Only the steady patter of rain overhead tapping off the last autumn leaves sounded. Grace was relieved. She even stopped for a moment to look up at the leaves still dropping in the rainfall, plummeting to the ground with more speed and less grace as they became covered in rain drops.

***

The in house tech had called with the plate numbers. They had finally caught the car mid dump of Chung on a highway toll camera. Chung's phone was still in the vehicle, giving them a dull signal to trace.

Tech was on the phone with Platt confirming the location of the vehicle. Just their luck, it had stopped at a high traffic diner two minutes up the road and it was still there. Tech stayed on the line as a precaution if the vehicle left before they retrieved Grace.

"It sounds like a trap." Ethan muttered from the back of the speeding car. "They wouldn't be stupid enough to pull over after dumping the body of a federal agent.' He looked at King to confirm his suspicion.

King nodded, looking behind them at the cavalcade of vans following Peters on his Frogger style leap though the highway's traffic.

"We have a team with us kid." King spoke quietly to Ethan afraid of waking Chung up in his state, crumpled across the backseat. "You just stay in the car okay?" He asked, looking to Ethan with a serious face.

Ethan nodded like a child, knowing that he would do whatever it took to get Grace back and that King's stern words wouldn't stop him from saving her if it came down to it. He quickly turned away from King's stoic stare and looked out the window at the passing cars. The car had fallen into an awkward silence and he could feel the eyes of the three agents burning into the back of his head as they glanced at him over their shoulders.

Soon, they too were pulling off the highway and onto the gravel parking lot for Tina's Diner. An old neon light flashed in the front window. *Open,* it read cheerfully blinking at a speed that was likely to cause a seizure for anyone sitting near it too long.

Peters pulled the car behind their suspect, blocking the car from escaping while sending a wave of brown water over its rear bumper. The gravel parking lot was riddled with craters filled with brown murky water from the storm. Looking at it through the foggy glass of the back window, it looked even and calm.

"Stay." King looked to Ethan as he exited the car with Peters and Platt. Ethan nodded, craning his neck to look in the back of the other car for Grace. His hand hovered on the doorknob, ready to pounce if she needed him regardless of King's orders.

King and Peters stood guarding with hands on their holsters, while Platt tinkered with a small kit opening the lock on the front door. With a click he pulled it open, pushing the automatic unlock button and the trunk release at the same time. The men rummaged through the car and all of its nooks and crannies.

King stood back watching the door to the diner, grasping at his holster tightly whenever the door chimed. After a thorough search of the car twice over, they came to the conclusion that Grace was nowhere to be found within it.

The men exchanged words outside where Ethan couldn't hear. He strained to see though the watermarks on the window, hoping to read their lips. Ethan failed to understand anything from their short chat. Soon after it had ended King stayed by the car and the other two walked into the diner like spies in an old bond movie.

Ethan popped the door open an inch, startling King. He turned to look at Ethan, eyes wary, "Where is she King?" He asked.

"Not here." King turned back, covering his eyes from the dripping rain. He stared intently at the doors to the diner, though they remained shielded from his vantage point.

"Is it the car?" Ethan prodded, fidgeting in the seat under the weight of Chung's unconscious body.

"Yup, blood and chloroform, this is it." King pointed to the car sitting quietly in the rain. "How's Chung?" He looked in the window to catch a glimpse of his partner's chest rising and falling in the pattern of a peaceful sleep.

Peters had left the car running so the heat would keep him comfortable. They had covered his bare arms over with a shiny blanket from the emergency kit. He looked like he was going to space.

"He looks the same." Ethan looked him over again lifting the shiny cover to see his bandages. Blood was seeping through most of his wrappings, mingling with the drying mud that plastered most of his body. He hadn't regained consciousness.

Ethan was no expert, but it didn't look all that promising. Still, he was breathing steadily. Ethan tried to smile at King encouragingly. He could tell from the look that crossed King's weary face that he didn't believe Ethan one bit.

Shots fired inside the diner. King bumped the door closed with his hip and pulled his gun out of the holster on his belt. He stood, waiting, pointed at the diner while water dripped down his face into his eyes. Ethan went white, he was trapped under Chung and King was against the door holding it closed. What if Grace was in there? He squirmed, trying to get out, to get into the diner, to get to Grace. But King was pressed up firmly against the door holding it shut and Chung lay heavily across the seat, too fragile to move.

***

Peters and Platt had walked into the diner, holding their guns at their waists. After a quick glance around the tiny place they had walked right to the only two men wearing suits.

At least they had made it easy.

As they approached the small booth the men occupied near the window the men looked up. They had both reached their hands under the table before Platt and Peters had a chance to stop them.

"Where is the girl?" Platt asked quietly in a calm voice, directing their gaze his own hand holding a loaded weapon. He knew that they were both doing the same under the dinner table. "Make it fast." He added twitching his brows as he jolted his arm, threatening a fast trigger finger to the two kidnappers.

The first man had drawn his own gun. Not fast enough for Platt who had restrained him by reaching out and twisting his arm. He redirected the gunfire to the roof of the diner.

The gunshot cracked through the small place, sending everyone ducking to the floor as plaster sprinkled down from the ceiling. Platt cracked the gun out of his hand and cuffed him while Peters was restraining his companion. They could hear whimpering under the table of the next booth.

Quickly flashing their badges at the other patrons and staff cowering under the bar, they dragged their suspects out into the parking lot towards a trigger hungry King.

An elderly man stood from his seat beside the diner's door. Unabashed by the commotion, he walked to the payphone to place a call.

***

Hart had tied up all the loose ends at the church and cabin personally, taking the time to relish in his own handy work after so many years of relying on henchmen.

When the link between the church and the cabin was found, the two fires would probably be blamed on hooligan teenagers like they always were. If the city ever found out that half the fires were started by him, they might start respecting their youth a bit more. He couldn't have that though: they made for easy scapegoats with their teen angst and utter defiance of authority.

Soon the fire department would be very busy and the crowd of teenagers that had already been drawn to the church would be a nice list of suspects. Many of them had previously been reported for breaking and entering at Hart's other warehouse locations, they all had records.

Now on route to his newest location, Hart wanted to ensure the preparations were complete before Grace arrived. Hart had a history of purchasing in bulk. He would wait for a recession to hit and then buy up several warehouses and abandoned buildings at one time, claiming to be restoring them. Every few years when he was done with a particular location (and hadn't had to burn it to the ground) he would call in a restoration team and bribe them into fixing it up cheap enough for him to resell and make a profit.

This newest property had been built specifically for Grace. She was going to be moved there in three weeks. After the recent series of events her move was being bumped up. Adding a video surveillance team at an alternate location was sure to alleviate some of the strain on his staff. He had initiated the changes earlier in the day before his initial trip to the church.

He expected the team to be in full reno-mode and to have the equipment up and running before Grace arrived. By the looks of the loose wires dangling all around him, he could tell they were appreciative of the extra few hours they were gaining from Grace's deliberate spunk.

His daughter was a born fighter; previous escape attempts had led him

ESCAPE

to draft his newest facility to accommodate people like her. The team of men around him were spinning in a chaotic tizzy. After noticing that Hart was in their midst, they had put down their coffees and started working with two hands with a gusto that was normally reserved for someone fighting for their life. And in this case, they were. Hart smiled at his worker ants, taking a seat at the open control panel.

The new building had been purchased at the same time as the church fifteen years ago. It had been reserved for Grace specifically, as her next home. Already fully staffed, it was a perfect fail-safe if his daughter had chosen to "act out" again. And after too many years at the church, Hart had started to get some flack from the town's mayor, waiting for the restoration of the historical building.

With an additional staff of video monitors and the seclusion of the forest, the hunting cabin should have been the first choice when Grace was moved into the church ten years ago. Hart however found something poetic in locking his only daughter away in a tower, like a sad little princess that would never be saved. He had been very wrong about the prospect of a knight in shining armour running aimlessly to her rescue.

Hart reached into his chest pocked as his phone buzzed, "Yes?" He answered dryly, and then, "I'll take care of it."

He sneered at his phone, frowning with a scowl that could curdle milk. Men scattered out of his way as he rose from his seat with force, snapping off an arm in the process. He stormed back out into the parking lot.

Getting back into his car, he turned the ignition and revved the engine, squealing back out onto the road. He would be back after he finished up some business. Hopefully this would be the last time he had to handle the mess on his own, or he was going to have to get his hands really dirty, and then re-hire. The thought made him smile.

LOST

Platt and Peters were discouraged to find that the men had expected to find an unconscious chloroformed Grace to be in the backseat of their filthy car.

Lazy on their part, the car was empty, save the wrappers and coffee stains. They seemed more terrified of their boss finding out than the FBI interrogation that was about to take place. They looked suspiciously at one another as they were taken away to the back of one of the black vans sitting in the diners lot, now buzzing with action. They were trying to corroborate their story before being questioned and had no idea what they were suppose to say.

Hart had hired a bunch of idiots. And now Grace could be anywhere. Platt and Peters stood at the hood of the suspects car and watched them clamouring into the back of the van before the doors were closed in on them.

The caravan of SWAT cars had entered the pond in the parking lot, taking over the puddle filled paradise like a trailer park of vans. Men stood outside their cars mingling and waiting for orders Ethan imagined them in plaid with beers in their hands, it completed the trailer park look.

Platt and Peters stepped back to allow a second team of men in to retrieve Chung. They clamoured into the small space, checking his vitals and ensuring that he hadn't sustained a neck or head injury before leaving him on Ethan's lap to go and get more supplies to move him.

King stood by, watching them closely trying to pass off his interest in their dialog as merely a business exchange. The look on his face displayed a great concern for their reaction to Chung's condition.

Stuck with another dead end, Platt was back on the phone with tech looking for a lead as to where Grace had gone. Dusk was falling and the autumn air grew cold as the storm washed over slowing to a light patter.

Ethan stared out the window, watching the light raindrops sending rings across the pond like puddle outside of his door. His legs had gone numb from the weight of Chung. He waited restlessly for the men to come back and transfer him to their medical van. From their light conversations earlier, he thought Chung might be doing alright, might even end up being okay.

He rested his head on the window staring out quietly. Ethan hoped that wherever Grace was, she was dry and warm.

***

Grace shivered as she continued through the woods. The trees were starting to thin out and she was hopeful civilization was getting closer. She stooped down by a small stream to take a drink of the murky water and stayed down for a couple of minutes to catch her breath.

Her clothes stuck to her back and legs, chafing from all the movement. She assumed it had been long enough that the men would have found her missing. Also that she had enough of a head start to give her the advantage. She stared into the trees looking back at the way she had come. By now Ethan and King would know she had been taken. She wished she still had Chung's phone.

And then she remembered that Chung was lying at the side of the road in the pouring rain. Guilt crept up into her, flushing her cheeks as her eyes filled with tears: *I'm sorry I couldn't save you.* She thought, wishing Chung could know how bad she felt that he had been thrown from the vehicle. He had been so nice to accompany her when the others were asked not to.

Thinking back on it, she could see how the whole situation was a setup. Why else wouldn't they let Ethan or Agent King stay with her? She frowned, watching the water trickle through the stream at her feet. Dipping her sore toes in to wash away some of the mud and caked on blood, she looked over her feet for splinters or broken bits of glass. She was sure that they were paining for a reason. They were covered in tiny nicks from the tunnels, the forest and the whole ordeal.

She would have been better off with a pair of shoes, but they weren't considered a necessity in the tower so she hadn't had any in ten years. She pulled a strip of fabric off of her tattered shirt under the thick coat. Ripping it into two; she wrapped the pieces around her feet and up her ankles to secure them. She was hopeful that they would protect her feet from some of the more painful forest elements. She zipped Chung's coat up tight; it hung loosely on her petite frame.

She hoped they would look to the road first for her trying to hitch-hike or call for help. They wouldn't expect her to run barefoot into the woods in the middle of a heavy rainstorm. It was likely the last place they would look for her. She felt a little bit safer. She just hoped that King and Ethan weren't looking too hard for her, they would never find her either. She would have to find them after she found help.

It was quickly growing dark. Grace looked to her surroundings before it was too dim to see. She knew that even if she knew how to start one, a fire would catch too much attention and it was far too damp out to find anything that would catch. So she settled for gathering piles of leaves to insulate her against the cool air.

She would rest for a couple of hours and then continue through the forest when the moon was high. She tucked her knees up and into Chung's large coat for warmth. The damp fabric was cool, but held nicely against the chill breeze that whipped through the trees above. Grace watched for the stars with heavy eyes, too wired to fall straight to sleep.

***

Peters was agitated, no one inside the diner had seen anything happen in the parking lot. Even two truckers who had been outside most of the afternoon smoking hadn't seen anyone except the two men exiting the car while they stood under a stoop sheltered from the storm.

Either the two suspects were lying and had passed her off to someone before going to the diner, or she had disappeared into thin air. The surveillance footage of them pushing Chung out of the car had shown the man shoving a pile of blankets down in the backseat. Peters was sure that was Grace.

He already had some men searching the road between Chung's drop and the diner looking for signs of an exchange, nothing had turned up yet. And it was unlikely they would find anything after the torrential downpour of the afternoon had wiped away almost all tracks in the area. They wouldn't even be able to use dogs to track her. Her scent was long gone. Wherever she was, she was off the radar and hopefully off of Hart's radar too.

A medical van had pulled up parallel with them to take Chung. They were checking his vitals in the back of the car again before moving him.

Ethan was gripping onto the back of the seat, as his legs screamed in agony. King could tell it wasn't good from the way they were checking and rechecking his vitals as they moved him onto the short stretcher pulled up to the open back door. They were taking him head first to get him into a neck brace and with the shiny blanket still tucked up over him he looked more like a robot than the partner King had been working alongside for the last six years.

King looked on, discouraged. They rolled away the stretcher and gently moved him over. With a sharp nod to King they closed the doors to their black van and drove away to take him in to the local hospital. King's eyes followed them out of the parking lot and onto the highway distractedly.

This rescue mission had gone from a crazy story they had joked about at the water cooler, into a very serious heist, attempting to pull the wool over the eyes of the largest criminal ring the district had ever had. Men like Hart took kidnapping very seriously, even if it was in an attempt to save his daughter from his own cruel hands.

Platt and Peters were deep in discussion, having just been pulled into this case earlier that day. They had a file open on the hood between them and were trying to take what King had told them earlier and piece together the severity of the situation.

A whole team had been taken out before they had been called in. So they had doubled their numbers and had two new reserve teams on standby nearby just in case. Mr. Hart was a notorious force, known among the men as an instigator of many of the regions criminal statistics. He had always managed to slide under the radar and they couldn't help but take extra precautions going up against him in the pursuit of his own daughter. Judging by Chung's sustained injuries, they couldn't be too cautious.

***

Hart pulled to the side of the road. Reaching back for a duffle bag tucked in the back of the car he quietly stepped out into the brisk autumn air, now sticky with the damp of the passing storm. He walked around his car and into the trees beside the highway, toting the awkward duffle bag over his shoulder.

He looked like a ruffled professor in his filth ridden suit, carrying a bag of books or papers to his students. Only the scowl that covered his otherwise lovely face gave him away as the evil thug he was. He trudged through the wet foliage, frowning as his suit became more dirty than it already was from all the other cover ups he had embarked on because of Grace's escape.

He was known for his pressed suits of prestigious quality, it had been far too long since he had ruined a thousand dollar suit on a trek through the wet forest foliage. It felt refreshing and at the same time it made him furious. He would burn the suit when he was done; it was full of evidence for sure and at the same time it was such a waste of a good suit. He paced twenty feet further and abruptly stopped under a tree dripping from the rain.

Dropping the duffle to the ground he knelt and unzipped the largest pouch. The ground beneath his knee sunk in to the mud giving him ample support from this position and keeping him steady. He grinned, *maybe the storm wasn't a waste after all* he thought smugly.

Inside the duffle bag an array of pieces sat piled, wrapped in thin cloth to protect them from rubbing against one another. Hart slowly and patiently assembled the pieces. Taking careful care to unwrap each piece like a present while keeping the cloths placed delicately to the side, laid out flat. The mummified pile of pieces slowly took the form of a military grade grenade launcher.

Looking over his completed work, Hart took extra care to secure each piece checking them twice over for imperfections before he attached the scope. He ensured his target was within range before loading the weapon. He took a moment to sit still in the trees watching through the scope at the scene before him. He had his timing just right when he pulled the trigger.

As the explosion blew hot air back into his emotionless face, Hart disassembled the hot weapon. Burning his suit and hands, he placed the steaming components back into the duffle taking the time to wrap each steaming piece in the heat resistant fabric only slightly blown by the breeze.

With a sharp zip of the bag, he slung it over his shoulder and turned his back to the heat of the explosion. He walked to his car, tossing the duffle back into the rear seats as he sped off down the highway back to the newest safe house to wait for Grace, or at least her body.

***

Ethan was pacing, trying to regain feeling in his legs. They screamed in agony, protesting his quick movements after being still for so long under agent Chung's weight. He fought through the pins and needles as he thought about the events that had taken place. *This has gone terribly wrong,* he thought.

He tried desperately to pinpoint where. He should have asked King to send one of his own men over that wall, not tried to be the hero. Things surely would have turned out differently had he not been longing for his romantic reunion with Grace. Hoping she would dash into his arms in slow motion, hair blowing in a gentle breeze. He shook the thought out of his head. How could he really have hoped for that? He was glad he hadn't found her tied to a post like she had found him. That would have broken his heart even more.

She hadn't even seemed to care that he was there. She was so determined to get out. He couldn't really blame her, in stories it always seemed like the princess was saved right away. No one talked about their time captive.

Real people had instincts, fight or flight reflexes. She was probably caught up in the escape even now...he hoped she was safe. Grace had always been an independent person, never relying on anyone else. How could she when her father had spent most of her childhood leaving her for weeks at a time with his business partners' families and nannies.

She had good instincts and after this many years captive, she had likely honed her loner gene to perfection. Wherever she was Ethan knew she wouldn't ask for help. She would fight as hard as she could to do it on her own and then try to save everyone else.

That could be a problem.

He could picture her, marching into a police station, covered in blood and muck, demanding to speak to the chief of police like they were old acquaintances. It almost made him chuckle. He gasped instead, running out of breath from all the pacing. His legs were on fire.

He stopped pacing to sit on the back bumper of Peters' car. Looking away from the diner into the small patch of dirty woods he thought of Grace as he remembered her. As kids they had played all kinds of games, her favourite had been saving the damsel in distress.

Grace had always played the hero and Ethan the princess. They would sneak into the woods behind her father's mansion and hide out for hours. Sometimes they would pretend they lived there and make furniture out of tree branches and leaves.

Standing, he stretched out his tired legs and walked to the edge of the woods, caught in his memories. He stared into the brush re-imagining himself a childhood where Grace hadn't gone away.

"Hey kid," Called King, "Ethan!"

Ethan turned from the trees to look back "Yah?"

"You find something over there?" King joked as he jogged over to Ethan.

Ethan looked down in confusion. Nestled in a discarded car tire, lay a plain clean cloth. It had been sheltered from the afternoon storm. Ethan picked it up, it smelled like chloroform. He looked back up to King, horror crossing his face as they both turned towards the forest in shock.

Behind them the diner twisted into a ball of fire. The explosion sent debris and fiery smoke billowing across the parking lot, knocking Ethan off his feet and into a tree. King spun around in time to see a swelling black cloud rising over the cavalcade of swat vans, blowing cars into them and toppling several of them over.

He hit the dirt, covering his head from the raining debris of the diner as it fell from the heavens in bits of smoke and fire.

DETONATE

Grace was awoken by a loud bang. Blinking she looked into the trees from where she had come. She could see the faint glow of a fire rising above the trees momentarily. It appeared as if a large fireball had emerged in the place where the diner had been. Bits of glowing embers fell back to the ground like fireworks. The forest was lit up like midday momentarily.

As she stared further into the trees she could still see the faint glow of what was probably a raging fire back at the diner. She knew it wasn't safe where she was any longer. Someone knew she was gone and it was likely her father, he had a bad habit of blowing things up or setting them on fire.

Grace stared for a moment in horror. Then she rose shakily from the leaf covering and began rushing blindly away from the amber glow that glimmered through the forest.

She slipped over rocks, up hills and down into creek beds. Her adrenaline kicked back in telling her to go faster, farther, as far away from the diner as she could get. She felt like she could run halfway around the world she was so suddenly filled with energy. The dim light in the forest gave her no trouble. As long as the glowing ember bursts were behind her she felt like she was going in the right direction. With every tree she stumbled into, a wash of water would fall from the treetops, refreshing, and re-energising her. She was running wildly. With the tree cover overhead, the night sky was providing her with little light.

She was once again left to rely on her senses of touch smell and sound to carry her forward into the dark night towards safety. She was oblivious to the other threats that waited further in the sanctuary of the dark looming forest.

Behind her the screams and screeches of car tires on the highway sounded like mice. She breathed heavily as she put more distance between her and the horror behind.

Stumbling, she fell with a sudden crash into a cold wet stream of water. Eyes glowed beside her. She looked past them to the smoulder behind her and began pulling herself forward. The tree line had broken, giving her minimal light to see her surroundings. Ahead of her lay a thick expanse of river.

Looking from left to right up the shore line, she could see no other option to cross over it. She lunged forward and dove in, gasping against the chill of the water as it rushed over her freezing her muscles instantly. She fought harder, propelling herself forward away from the fire and the waiting beasts at the shoreline. She fought her way towards the dark forest on the other side.

***

Hart had arrived at the building again and toured the facilities, twice. He was expecting more progress in the hour he had been gone. Wires still hung from the ceiling like streamers at a party.

He marched through the scrabbling crowd of workers, immensely displeased with their performance. They looked as exhausted as he should feel after running about all day. He hoped the explosion had had some time to settle down back at the diner, he was tempted to send his useless crew there to walk through the fire. He knew he couldn't afford to expend of too many resources in one day. So he settled in to watch them work like bees building a perfect hive. Fury washed over Hart, he was not usually such an emotional man. That day however, his life work hung in the balance and incompetence was not acceptable. He crushed a Styrofoam cup of coffee in his hand. The hot coffee poured down his hand onto the concrete floor pooling in a steaming mass.

Hart brushed his hand off onto his soiled suit pants and reached for his cell. Two rings and a raspy voice answered.

"Yes."

"Phase three. Fail and you will all be eradicated." The steel in Heart's eyes translated through the phone, he could hear the brief pause on the other end.

"Yes, Sir"

With a click, he tucked the phone back away. Walking to the control room for a third time, he was ready to make some changes. If Grace made it out of this she was going to pay. His team looked up rapt with attention. They knew better than to keep him waiting.

***

On the other side of the river, Grace had pulled herself free of the flowing water. She had no idea if she had washed down river while swimming for her life or not.

Grace was starting to feel exhausted. She fought past it restlessly as the chills set in. She began to shake violently, her teeth chattered. Brushing the damp leaves off of her legs she stood, jogging on the spot to get some warmth back in her tiny body. Fighting to keep her eyes open she looked back across the river. She could see only a dim glow in the distance, over the peaceful top of the immense forest sprawled out before her.

Waiting until the moon was high was no longer an option. She would be frozen by then. The temperature was dropping too quickly. Trying to remember which way she had come from, she put the light glow behind her. Grace turned and continued on her path further into the woods. She tried to maintain a straight line away from the now dim light of the burnt out diner, hoping not to get lost.

The incline became steep as the night settled in. She slipped on the wet floor of foliage, gripping trees for support. The slippery moss gave way on her more than once, sending her back down the hill several times before she reached the summit of the steep thing.

Soon, Grace was sure she was lost. She pondered about starting a fire for warmth and just setting in for the night; then remembered she didn't know how and that it was probably still too damp out to do much anyway.

In the distance she could hear wolves howling. She stopped, trying to determine if they were on her side of the river. She was unable to tell, but stopping for the night was sounding more dangerous by the moment.

Grace stooped down, feeling along the ground until she came back up with a large stick. She would feel slightly better about being in the dark spooky woods if she thought she had a weapon. Grace just hoped she didn't run into the pack of wolves. She looked out across the forest before her.

Relief washed over her as she saw the lights of a city ahead. It looked far off in the distance, but it gave her a direction to aim for. Placing the lights directly in her path, she began to walk again. Forward, back down the hill using her new walking stick for support, she stumbled a little less on the way down.

***

King jogged to Ethan at the edge of the woods. He was holding something and looking to the trees like a spaceship had landed. He looked rigid and pale. The blast had blown him over and he lay there unmoving with a wild look still plastered across his face.

Behind him, black billowing smoke wrapped itself around the parking lot, choking anyone who had managed to avoid the initial blast. The puddles in the lot reflected the chaos of swirling reds and blacks as the fire raged on uncontrolled in the debris of the diner. A disarray of survivors ran wildly across the lot, looking for cars and keys, screaming and weeping in an eerie melody of grief.

Several of the SWAT cars had been blown over from the impact of other cars and debris. Others were missing chunks out of their sides. The new cars pulling in were moving in slow motion avoiding pedestrians and debris. King ignored the scene behind him, focusing on the unmoving body of Ethan at the base of the woods.

"Kid, what have you got there? Are you okay?" King asked, coming up slowly trying not to spook Ethan in his comatose state.

He stepped around in front of Ethan, cutting off his glassy eyed gaze into the mysterious beyond. Ethan barely started. Looking to King for a moment, his gaze returned sharply into the trees. He looked lost in his thoughts. King shook him lightly trying to retain his focus.

King was splattered with mud and debris from the burning diner. Lucky for the vans that had absorbed most of the blow, he and Ethan were left unharmed. The team had suffered few injuries. Inside the diner however, was another story.

The fire department had been called. Police were already speeding into the lot sending up plumes of water as they hit the large full puddles and their brakes swerving to avoid hitting the screaming masses at the same time. The lot was quickly turning into a zoo. The exit had become blocked with debris and there was a long line of cars waiting to get out, blocking the only way in.

"Grace..." Ethan trailed off looking through King and into the trees for answers. He clutched his hands tightly together pulling on the fabric, shielding it from the smoke.

King tugged the cloth from his hand, noting the clean linen under the flickering street post that had lit above the two of them suddenly. Under the luminescent blue glow the cloth shone like a beacon. He sniffed it, glad he had held it away from his face, for the residual smell of chloroform lingered. It was apparent, even over the overwhelming burning smoke that clung to everything on the lot.

"Where did you find this?" He asked Ethan, looking to the filthy muddy mess at their feet, and then into the forests edge with curiosity. Ethan pointed at his feet to a filthy tire settled among low bushes and wrappers. The cloth hadn't been there long. It was very likely that Grace had passed by dropping it on her way.

"Peters!" King called over his shoulder. Turning, he ran to meet agent Peters by the car. King was exuberant, swing the cloth through the air like a puppet and spinning the most elaborate story.

Ethan stood dumbfounded at the edge of the woods, looking at the tree he had fallen into earlier with curiosity. If Grace was out there in the trees would she have gone far, or was she sitting close by injured and unable to call for help?

Ethan was about to climb into the trees to look for her when King finished talking to Peters. A small crowd had gathered around the two of them. They exchanged words and three of the men followed King back to Ethan.

They carried cases with them and stopping short at the tire. They began rooting through their cases, taking samples and looking for tracks. Flashlights quickly complimented the overhead luminosity, lighting up the area like a UFO landing site. Ethan stood watching them, looking himself for anything that would indicate Grace had passed through. The lights flashed into the woods, clinging low to the ground.

It was then that he saw it. He began pointing dramatically in hopes that the forensics would see. A small, bare footprint etched as clear as day in a small patch of mud beyond the tree line. Barely visible by the dim lights overhead. Forensics called more men over. Ethan backed away to catch up with King. He had hope.

VULNERABLE

Hart sat in Grace's new room inspecting the changes. He inspected every inch of the small space looking for faults that she may pick out as opportunities to escape. The new room was kept to a bare minimal.

Linoleum rolled floors left no cracks to be picked at. It had ten foot ceilings with solid white walls. The small washing area was a step up from her space in the tower, with a showerhead and drain in the floor but no curtains. The bed was bare, with no sheets. She had now lost that privilege after proving her skills at knot tying. He couldn't afford to let anything happen here.

The door was sealed into the wall, invisible from the interior. Her meals would be conveyed in through a miniscule trap door. Hart was quite pleased with how the room had turned out. Looking up he could see the specs where the cameras had been installed. There would be more in the outer rooms, giving Hart a chance to check in on his guards at any time to make sure they were working to their full potential; very little room for error. It was nearly perfect, save for the specimen that should be confined inside.

Waiting for the third team to bring her in was putting a strain on Hart. He was growing restless and fatigued; only his rage was keeping him going.

Had she not been his own daughter, she would have been dead years ago.

The new room was state of the art. With integrated cameras that would capture her every movement, motion detectors and two way glass in all the mirrors.

Essentially the room was a small square in the centre of a large room. It was to be monitored on all sides by a team of four. A second team was located at the end of the gated property. They were in charge of watching the grounds with surveillance of the guard station in case of emergency.

Hart knew that once Grace was in there, she would never see the outside world again. He smugly relished in the fact that his secrets would die there with her, locked away from the world forever.

***

King had sent a team to the town behind the diner. Oneida was over 20 miles away and separated from the diner by an expansive forest and creeks that broke off from the large river that crossed through the national forest.

If Grace was alive and out there she could be lost forever. That was if she could survive with all the predators already lurking in the trees. They would scour the forest from both sides for signs that Grace had passed though. They had planned on sending in a team of dogs to search for any scent she may have left after the storm. But with so little to go on and the local wolves, it seemed unlikely that they would pick up on anything useful, so they were left out of the trip.

Day was soon to break again and Ethan had fallen asleep waiting in the back of an abandoned car. Some of the men were taking a break in the broken vans sitting around the lot waiting to be towed, while they passed the time until further instruction was given. King stood by a sleek black car watching the woods, hoping the case would break before he did.

He and Chung had been hoping to crack the case. The publicity would have sent them to Washington for sure. Right now King didn't know if

Chung would ever go home, Washington seemed farther away than ever.

King sat on the trunk of the car and stared off into the dwindling night sky. He pondered if there were a faster way to find Grace, or if they even needed her to close the case.

Sure she was a major piece of evidence, but after all the action Hart had been involved in over the last few days he was sure to have slipped up somewhere. The man couldn't be perfect. King called a free agent over.

"Send a team of analysts into the woods over there." He pointed to the direction the blast had come from. "See if you can't find something useful."

The agent nodded to him, taking off with a purpose. Quickly he had gathered a team of five or so and was rounding up some equipment when King turned away to the expanse of forest that Grace had taken off into.

Smokey fire still raged behind King, warming him in the cool damp air. Firefighters and paramedics seemed to rush past him in slow motion as he retraced his steps from that day. It was hard to believe that only twenty four hours ago he had been waiting for Ethan and Grace to pop through a trap door, not sure if he had taken a real case or a hoax. He felt the stitches in his arm from the gunfight at the cabin, if only Chung were so lucky.

***

Grace was tiring quickly, pausing again to drink from a small stream as the sun rose. She fumbled through the pockets of Chung's jacket finding a pack of wet mint gum. She tore into a piece greedily, saving the wrapper in her pocket, just in case. The forest was disorienting, Grace found herself keeping her eyes closed to help her stay in a straight line. Holding her hands before her she walked calculatedly around trees and obstacles. She winced as her foot struck a sharp rock, tearing through her fabric wrap; it stung as she began bleeding into the already saturated cloth.

She had a feeling that she was veering ever slightly off course and could end up wandering in the woods for weeks. After stopping to catch her breath for a third time, she saw a low lying branch in a tree ahead. She stooped down to retie the cloth on her feet and then climbed the tree with the enthusiasm of a child on a jungle gym.

The damp mossy branches slipped under her touch and she had to climb more slowly than she would have liked, due to the awkwardness of the heavy coat draped from her shoulders. The branches grew farther apart as she wove through the crevices up to the top of the tree line. When she could see above the surrounding trees she scoured the area for the lit up city she had seen the night before. It was more difficult to pinpoint in the light morning air.

After a few moments she saw it tucked away in an alcove of trees in the distance. It appeared desolate and she couldn't make out a road from her vantage point in the treetop. It was still a few hours away, Grace estimated it would take most of her strength to get there.

She chose to continue moving before her hunger became intolerable. She would rest when she got there. Shrugging back down through the tree, careful of her footfalls, Grace reached the bottom and picked her walking stick back up. In the morning light it was less startling in the dense forest, she was sure she would see a predator from the distance now that it was light out. Still she clung to the stick for protection, knowing that even if there were a predator she couldn't fight it off with her bare hands. She put the direction of the town before her and walked on, thinking only of her usual morning protein shake, willing herself to keep going.

***

King's phone buzzed, waking him from a light sleep. Sitting in the reclined passenger seat of their replacement black car, he answered in a thick voice.

"Hello?"

It was Chung. He had woken up in the hospital and was going in for surgery on his shoulder. Relief washed over King, as he smiled into the phone. "You tell him to hang in there, alright." King joked into the receiver.

Now awake, and with the morning sun glaring in his eyes preventing him from dozing back off, King exited the car and walked to a small huddle of men around one of the less damaged vans.

King had already given a detailed account of the events of the previous day for their records and recalculation. Since the last time he had checked they had devised several new protocols and were dividing the remaining men into teams to begin the recapture mission.

The team that King had sent out earlier had returned with bags of evidence that had been sent in for analysis. Hopefully something in there would be enough to start their case against Hart. King loudly volunteered to join the group heading into Oneida to provide backup for the forest search that was already taking place there.

He had a feeling that Grace was a resourceful girl and would amazingly turn up somewhere in the forest, kicking and biting. She seemed to have quite a bit of spunk in her. Platt and Peters had already volunteered for the same group, making them a team of three. They listened for their instructions from the agent in lead at head office. With the damage that had already been done; King had been removed of his 'officer in charge' title and was stuck conforming to the duties of lower ranking squad men.

Walking back to their car the men remained silent, all sure that they would be the ones to find the girl alive. Platt tossed himself into the passenger seat next to Peters who had greedily taken up the wheel again.

"Should we ditch the kid?" He asked referring to the still unconscious Ethan tucked into the backseat. King shook his head, moving Ethan's legs over to climb in beside him.

"Leave him, he'll cause too much trouble here." He looked over to the smouldering diner, thinking how lucky they were to have been outside. In the last few hours firefighters had finally managed to contain the blaze, leaving a smouldering charred pile where the building had once been. A crew of men were now cordoning off the building remains with fencing so they could investigate further into the cause.

King could see over his shoulder the fire department conversing with a team of forensics who wanted in to see the wreckage. The site would be busy for weeks. He rolled his eyes at the crowds of curious people parking at the side of the road on their way out. They were all hoping to get a look at the diner that had imploded in a ball of smoke and fire. And that was the last thing they needed; a media frenzy.

***

Hart was growing impatient with waiting. She was sure to turn up soon. No remains had been found in her likeness at the diner and his undercover man had indicated that she had previously escaped into the woods nearby. It was a shame that she had not chosen his direction.

He couldn't help but imagine the scenario where he had caught her and made her watch as he blew up the diner with her precious Ethan inside. It truly would have been a victory, but he would settle for revenge. And as of yet her whereabouts were unknown. Hart was painfully aware that she could not be allowed to be found, even if it were just her corpse.

It would lead to an inquisition into her death ten years previously and he would be just as liable as in the scenario where she escaped with the FBI unharmed.

Hart ran his hand over Grace's new bed one last time, now refreshed after a quick nap. In a deep menacing voice he demanded. "Open the door" Looking up to several of the cameras as he marched across the room where a section of wall swung open instantly, allowing Hart to step out into the antechamber.

He began to examine the equipment out of boredom and spite. The wires that had dangled into his face earlier were now tucked away neatly, leaving a clean pristine environment. It looked advanced in its technological savvy. The thought of his daughter being trapped in there like zoo animal, watched over twenty-four-seven gave him a reason to smile while he waited for his lackeys to bring him a coffee.

Sometimes he would take satisfaction in timing them while they were running around doing his errands. In that moment he was not in the mood for compassion, "*coffee.*" He snipped into the quiet air, sitting in a vacant chair at the control panel. He looked over the switches and dials with pleasure, holding his hand out expectantly.

Exactly five seconds later a hot cup of coffee slid into his hand.

EXPOSED

Grace was running out of steam, falling from one tree to the next, clinging on for support. She had long since expired all of the gum in Chung's coat and had not found anything else edible. She stopped to sniff at some small berries, not sure if she should go for it or not.

She was sure that they were poisonous because she had never seen them before. Yet she was ravenous and was ready to eat just about anything. She settled for chewing on her lip as she fell forward, crawling through the trees for a stretch before regaining her footing with the help of her walking stick.

She hadn't passed a stream in hours and was dehydrated and disoriented. She climbed a second tree to verify the town was still within her path. This time the tree was more difficult to venture into, given her delirious state. She fumbled, falling several times from the second branch before reaching the top. Looking out through the tree, it took her a few moments to remember what she was looking for.

It was then that Grace started fearing for her life. She knew that she needed to get out of the woods fast or she wasn't going to make it out at all. In the blazing mid day sun the houses appeared like a mirage on the horizon ahead of her.

Grace was having trouble keeping her eyes open. To keep herself awake she sang the "ABC's" over and over again. Keeping pace, she took a step every time she whispered a letter into the abundant tree-filled landscape that stood between her and the city that she had named Freedom.

The sun blinded her as it snuck through bare patches of branches overhead, blaring into her tired eyes. The forest had come to life around her in the early morning hours. At some points she felt like the animals were following her, trying to make sure she left their home intact. She stopped to listen to the birds a couple of times, sure that she could understand them.

If the houses weren't close enough, Grace was likely going to go mad. "A...B...C..." She muttered under her breath, pressing her bleeding feet into the earth with each syllable.

***

Peters made record time, speeding to Oneida like he thought he could beat the reconnaissance team there. The other team had left four hours earlier and were already in the woods scouring for clues and trails.

That didn't slow Peters down. He had a look about him like he was behind the wheel of the DeLorean and expected to break the barrier between times at any second. He wove through the cars like they were pylons marking his route.

The road was narrow with no shoulder, giving him less room for error. Twice he had nearly run a car into the forest and looking briefly in his rear-view mirror he would whistle as the car pulled itself back onto the road.

They had stopped briefly before plowing onto the highway to grab a bag full of burgers and a tray of coffee to bring them all back to the land of the living. Peters had continued driving at neck breaking speeds one handed while his other hand pressed a burger into his face. Platt sat gripping the door hysterically trying to remain calm for the two minutes it took Peters to devour three burgers and a coffee.

Ethan sat quietly in the back seat, eating, afraid that if he said a word he would be kicked from the vehicle and unable to help Grace. He shrunk into the seat, willing the agents not to see him. None of them had even so much as glanced at him since he had woken up in the moving backseat, half sprawled across an uncomfortable looking agent King. He stared out the window like a statue with a full mouth, watching the reflections of the agents in the glass. Ethan was not sure where they were going, he tried to pick up a tidbit from the landscape outside. It didn't seem familiar to him. Still he hoped that was the forest Grace had gone in to earlier and that they were not taking him away from her.

King and Platt made light conversation in the background. Comparing academy experience and cases they had worked, partners they had had and other useless information while Peters wound through the one lane traffic like a lunatic playing a car chase game with their lives. Ethan listened intently, straining to hear over the manic car horns that were talking to Peters with waving fingers as he plowed several cars off the road.

King and Platt had mentioned Oneida, Ethan remembered going there on a field trip to the national park as a child with Grace. It wasn't far off from Jamestown where the cabin had been. Ethan returned his gaze to the window, reflecting afternoon light into his eyes. He squinted to see the forest better. Finding Grace was going to be like finding a needle in a haystack.

Taking the back road was supposed to get them there faster and it gave them an opportunity to look into the vast woods for signs of unusual behaviour within their confines. The trees lined the side of the road, tall with thick foliage in the autumn bloom. Ethan could see a few feet into the forbidding trees. He gazed, desperate for a sign of movement or anything that would indicate Grace was close.

Then they crossed a large river and Ethan caught a glimpse of the expanse of the forest along the shore line. Trees trailed off past his line of vision. His heart leapt into his throat. Even if Grace knew where she was going, it would take her forever. And with a river to cross, she was unlikely to be in Oneida on the other side.

Ethan looked to King and Platt, who had abruptly paused their conversation to look out at the river and expanse of trees that daunted their chances of finding Grace soon. Ethan could tell they felt the same as him; they were going the wrong direction.

Unabashed, Peters drove on madly, swerving around an incoming car.

***

Grace found herself at the top of a rolling hill on her knees gasping for breath with white dots darting before her eyes. She was losing consciousness. Fighting against it, she clawed her way up a tree to look forward. Peering ahead through the trees, she could see that she would be closing in on a house shortly.

The sun was hanging low in the sky indicating the night closing in on her again. The orange glow hung low over the house, lighting it up like a beacon in the distance. She stared at it in wonder as the glass in the windows reflected the forest back to her. It reminded her of when she was on the other side of the glass looking out. In that moment she almost wished she still were, and then she shook some sense into herself.

Trees were thinning out. She had worn her voice hoarse mumbling the alphabet to keep her pace. She now only counted each step in her head, just thinking of random numbers as her tired feet paced the rough terrain. Her feet were raw from the days on them in unfamiliar environments. She longed for a pair of shoes, or a soft surface to walk on. Her sore soles missed the worn soft wood of the tower floor. As she raced through the trees towards her destination she felt like she was running in slow motion.

A fence loomed at the bottom of the steep cliff ahead, relief washed over her.

Grace paused at the edge of the precipice her clothing clung to her in the gentle cold breeze. She looked down on the house in the distance. The sun hung on the horizon. From there she could see for miles, further into the small town before her. It looked quiet and at peace. Grace was confused for a moment by its aloofness. The town made no noise. No streetcars whizzed down the streets. No children laughing, no one talking. It was as if the town was empty.

The lights in the house ahead were intimidating. She considered for a moment staying and living out the rest of her life in the woods. Somewhere inside she knew she would have to keep running if she ever wanted to stop.

She set her shoulders and grabbed at a tree branch to begin the climb down. Grasping for tree roots and rocks she slowly clamoured to the bottom. Grace looked down and judged the fall before letting go a few feet from the ground. She landed with a sharp shock up both of her shins beginning a run towards the bottom of the gentle hill below her.

Grace slammed into the fence after building momentum on her downhill jog. She stood slowly, winded and began to trace the fence with her hand. Walking towards the front of the property, she hoped someone would be home.

***

Platt and Peters had taken up residence outside the car that now sat parked outside the national park. It idled silently in a small parking lot, next to the analysts' van.
A team was scouting for signs of Grace in the forest while they sat parked, waiting for the signal to either help or leave. The initial excitement of the rescue had long since gone for Ethan. Leaving him unnerved and on edge. He wanted to curl up and sleep to save his energy, but every time he closed

his eyes he felt guilty that Grace didn't have the same option. Wherever she was, she was running for her life. And no matter how hard he tried to stop thinking about it, he couldn't let the feeling go that she was more tired and deserving of sleep than he.

"She's not out there is she?" Ethan looked to King, who sat restlessly tapping his foot next to Ethan, staying in the car for warmth and possibly to avoid the awkward conversations Peters and Platt were having outside of the car. To Ethan, they looked like a married couple bickering about what was for dinner.

"No." King answered plainly, turning his gaze from Platt and Peters towards the edge of the tree line, growing darker by the second.

Ethan looked out at Platt who was pacing by the tree line. He appeared to be having a heated discussion about the same thing, whether or not Grace was going to be found.

"Anything from the other side?" Ethan asked, referring to the patch of forest back by the diner. He looked up to King expectantly, knowing that he had recently taken a hushed call outside the car.

"Her footprints were washed away by the storm. Even the dogs can't track her." King breathed heavily over his cold coffee. Shaking his head he leaned back into the seat behind him. "If she's out there, she's probably lost."

He looked guilty, like he had forced her into the woods. Ethan could tell that he felt like he *had* forced her when he sent her with the fake agents. He fell silent again in the back of the stuffy car watching the sky turn deep violet over the trees.

***

Grace had walked the perimeter of the house trailing her fingers along the wooden fence and rough stonework. She struggled to stay upright as she fought her way to the front door. A porch light glowed across a worn stone walkway.

Lights shone through the covered windows casting long shadows towards Grace as the sun stopped glowing on the horizon, leaving her basking in only the lights from inside the house. Grace stepped up to the front door and knocked, faintly making contact with the solid wooden oak of the entranceway.

It reminded her of the oak doors her father use to close in her face reminding her cruelly every day that she was not to hear what happened behind them. His office had been a forbidden place in her family home and that had only led to her own curiosity seeing her over the threshold more than once.

She stared blankly at the door closed in her face like in her memory. With the last of her strength and years of welled up anger, she began pounding at it like she wanted to break it down before her.

A shuffling began inside moving cautiously towards the front, likely wary of her flailing arms pounding at the door that was shaking it in its frame. Voices sounded and then the door swung open, slowly, just enough for someone to peek out cautiously before opening it the whole way.

Grace stood face to face with a teenage boy. He rose almost a foot taller than her and his long un-kept hair dangled into his eyes. The rocker tee he sported was in a state of disrepair, crumpled like it had been balled up on the floor for weeks. He looked her over with wide eyes.

"Shit…" He muttered turning to yell, "Mom!" over his shoulder. He backed away from the open door retreating into the small house like a deer caught in headlights as he continued to look at Grace like she was a zombie there to eat his brains.

A woman appeared at the door, tired looking and obviously frustrated that her son had called her over. She took one look at Grace and turned back to him in horror.

"James, call 911, tell them we need help, *now!*" She pushed him back into the house with urgency ,"Go." She yelled after him as he stumbled off, looking back in confusion.

She took Grace gently by the arm and guided her into the house. She looked out across the driveway with concern before locking and dead-bolting the door behind them.

"What happened honey?" The woman asked, softly leading Grace to a small kitchen table. Looking over Grace's tangled hair and tattered clothing. She looked back to the door and the trail of mud and blood that Grace had unwittingly trailed into her home. She seemed curious as to what the strange girl had been through to be so worn.

Grace had forgotten how rough she must look. Dried blood mingled with dirt on her rotting tattered clothes. Her hair was matted to her face in a disarray of dirt and debris. *These people must think the worst.* And they were probably still far off from how bad it actually was.

"Oh..." Grace began, startled. She was not sure what exactly to tell her, or where to start.

"Take your time dear." She continued rushing around the kitchen pulling food and glasses towards the cluttered table in a hurried panic. She began clearing things off of the table onto the couch across in the living room and then filling the table back up with food. It seemed like anything edible she found was quickly placed on the table.

Grace ravenously devoured a glass of water. With an unquenchable thirst, she reached for the pitcher to refill it. The women stopped her and poured Grace a fresh glass looking at the girls shaking hands with pity.

WANTED

It was quarter after ten when Jay took the call, direct from his girl at dispatch. He had five minutes to get in there, grab the girl and get out before the real police arrived.

The thrill of the chase was only accentuated by the short time frame. It was going to be one of his most intense missions to date, even trials run by the team to keep them fresh rarely got them going so quick. Jay signaled to his team, they were ready for action. It had been years since they had run a live capture. Their practice scenarios to keep the big guys happy had even gotten easier over the years out of boredom. In those scenarios they only had to prove that they were not going soft after all these years, always sharp on their toes.

They were two minutes out when the call came; already waiting in Oneida hoping she would come through. His other team headed back to Hart, useless from their setup on the other side of the river. In situations like this it was always better to have two teams laying in wait, just in case it ended up being a rush job.

Racing to the address in their sleek black imitation FBI cars their adrenaline began pumping. He parked his car around the corner as a backup, just in case scenario where they had to sneak her around the block.

It was a failsafe they had used for years. Jay raced around the corner where his team had already kicked in the door and fanned into the house, taking over the small space in a matter of seconds.

Grab the girl and go.

That was it.

The family could try and explain it to the police after; they would look crazy anyway. The house had an easy layout. The kitchen and living room were both right inside the front door, with a small walkout to the backyard from the kitchen that was easily secured.

She was sitting in the kitchen with a mother and son. Jay grabbed for her arm as his men circled around to cover all the entrances. She swung a mug at his wrist and blocked him. Standing with swift movement, the girl was preparing to fight the men off.

She looked shaky and frail, like a leaf blown through the wind. All covered in brown mud and tufts of orange hair peeking through, she looked easy enough to take down.

Taking her lead, the mother and son had begun to hit and kick, protecting themselves and inadvertently Grace. She stood between the two, using them like shields. Jay hated fighting the unsuspecting comrades of his targets. He usually went for another route when it came to that.

Dropping a smoke grenade, Jay pulled his mask down. This had to go faster if they hoped to outmaneuver the police. He reached for the spot the girl had stood and grabbed her from under the arms. She flailed and kicked at him, dragging her body and squirming to get away. He held tighter, pulling her with ease.

He began to drag her out of the house, commanding his men follow. At the foyer he looked down into the terrified eyes of the mother, not Grace. She bit at him, clawing at his arm while she screamed garbled words in terror. He dropped her hard on the floor and marched back into the kitchen.

"Where is she?" He grunted into the smoke racing back into the house frantically.

Men groped through the room, searching for her through the mist. They came up empty handed. She was gone like the smoke now dissipating in the kitchen air.

"Out back." Jay demanded, pointing to the sliding back doors off of the kitchen. "Surround the house and wait." He commanded, slipping past the screen and into the night.

They would wait out the police and continue looking. And in the event the police found her first, they would swoop in and take their target before they could call for backup.

She would be theirs again.

Sirens began to sound as the last of the men evacuated, disappearing into the trees quieter than the rustling of the leaves in the wind.

***

Grace couldn't breathe. The smoke hung thick in the kitchen air. While the cloud grew she ducked to the floor, crawling under the table. There was yelling and dragging, it sounded like they were all leaving in a hurry.

She scurried out of the kitchen and up a set of stairs. She soon found herself in a bathroom. Slowly closing the door over and locking it, she left the light off. The sounds from downstairs were chaotic. The smoke clung to her insides as she tried desperately to catch her breath as quietly as possible.

She was sure they would notice soon that she had gone missing. She just needed one more moment to pull herself together. Quietly she climbed into the bathtub, clutching at her sides as she slowly drew the curtains around herself, giving her a small sense of security for at least a moment or two.

Sirens sounded outside the house. Grace could see their lights flashing through the shower curtain. Pulsing through the images of flowers and birds that dotted the fabric surrounding her, the mesmerizing blues and reds were hypnotic.

The porcelain was cold and as she looked around at the familiar set up she realized it had been years since she had even seen a bathtub. She ran her fingers along the smooth surface in envy. Grace silently reached for the bottle of shampoo sitting across the tub. She smelled the calm lavender with enthusiasm.

She missed her old life and there she was sitting in a tub cowering from her last chance to get it back. She blacked out for a moment, lost in a memory from her childhood.

Grace could remember having a big bubble bath, while her mother was getting ready for some big party in the bathroom mirror. The tub was filled with bubbles and she couldn't have been older than four. The tub had spilled over with bubbles and water. Her mother had looked to her with a warm smile, walked over and turned the water off, tossing a towel on the spill lazily, "Grace," She had chided happily, "you might just be a mermaid." Grace had smiled and splashed in the bubbles happily pretending she was, while her mother continued getting ready.

That was the last time she had seen her mother, she wondered if she too had been locked away by her father.

Grace didn't know how much time had passed. She needed to get out of there before they found her. In a startled panic, she slipped from the tub and walked to the small high window.

Looking out from the second story she could see the hill behind the house, beyond the fence, where she had come in. Shapes moved up the hill, into the woods. At least ten bodies surrounding the house, slipping into cover amongst the trees. She would have to wait it out a bit longer.

More sirens sounded in the distance.

ESCAPE

***

Peters was on the phone with tech. A call had come in from the Oneida police department about a battered girl needing medical attention. The address was backing onto the forest.

The closest team had already been sent in. Peters and Platt were following with King. Their team in the forest had added the new location to their GPS and were walking in that direction, still looking for Grace's trail.

They left the second car there, piling back into the sleek black of their company vehicle and onto the winding roads of North Tennessee.

Peters sped back onto the highway. Taking the next exit they began winding through the small town towards the properties closest to the adjoining forest.

The desolate town sat mostly silent in the late autumn evening. Eerily staring back at them were closed store windows and vacant lots. Sirens sounded in the distance echoing in the silent streets. They drove towards the sound on the empty streets. It was like being in a ghost town.

Ethan, still in the back, woke with a start as they plowed over a speed bump. Pretending to have been awake the whole time he sat up wiping a trail of drool from his chin. King looked to him with a raised knowing eyebrow and a smirk on his face.

"Hey, where are we going? Did you find her?" Ethan's tone quickly jumped from groggy to alert as he noticed the speed they were driving.

Wind whipped in from the rolled down drivers window as Peters plunged onto a dark street. The breeze slapped Ethan's hair against his forehead and it slowly became un-plastered after his stint of sleep against the window. He looked out to the eerie town, befuddled as to how Grace could have ended up there.

"You *need* to stay in the car." King reminded him. The air fell silent as the car sped forward. Ethan pulled his lips tight and reached for a seatbelt, nodding his acknowledgement to King. He turned to the window. Looking out into the haze he rolled his eyes. King could treat him like a child all he wanted. Ethan was a grown man and would do whatever he wanted.

***

The police had arrived on the scene followed closely by the team Peters had called. After exchanging information with the lead officer and waiting for them to call their own back up in, they proceeded together into the house, three agents and two badges.

The kicked in door clung uselessly from a hinge, waving them forward into the disarray of the tiny cottage home at the edge of town. The smoke had nearly cleared from the kitchen where they found a mother and son huddled under the table. Objects were strewn about in a manner that suggested a tussle had broken out resulting in them hiding in the cloudy room under the table.

"They wanted the girl." The mother sobbed, clutching her son to her after one of the officers knelt next to her showing her his badge.

She shook terribly, clinging to the fabric of her son's rumpled shirt like a security blanket. Her shirt was ripped at the collar and around them an array of kitchen utensils and mugs lay scattered and broken on the floor.

The boy seemed shaken up as well. Cuts on his hands and blood under his fingernails showed his determination as he held his mother close, looking to the officers with steely eyes.

The struggle in the home was obvious and the kettle still squealed at a boil on the stovetop across from them. A second officer walked over and took the kettle off the burner. The whistle quickly died down as he moved it over.

"Did they get her?" He asked turning to the cowering family beneath the table.

"I don't know. There was smoke everywhere." The woman sobbed.

Slowly climbing from beneath the safety of her kitchen chairs, she held her son tight by the arm as he joined her in a huddle.

The boy shook his head firmly. "She's still here, they were pretty pissed about it too." He looked back at his mother, wrapping his arm around her tighter. "I think they'll come back for her. Get us out of here." He begged, slowly inching his mother out from under the table and up into a chair.

For a teenager he seemed to have grown into a whole lot of responsibility in one hour. Knowing to move his mother slowly to prevent more shock to her system, he stood behind her holding her shoulders. "Get us out of here." He repeated to the team of men standing in the kitchen.

The men nodded in agreement.

"Check the house." The first officer commanded, staying by the boy and his mother. He pointed to the others to get moving.

The team split into two: police and agents, to search the house.

SHIELDED

Grace huddled beside the bathtub watching the flickering lights in the window. She could hear noises downstairs, heavy footsteps and voices. She could hear weeping as the footfalls stopped momentarily and she wondered if the family downstairs was alright.

She felt a tug of guilt for bringing her problems crashing through their front door. The footsteps started up again, circling around the downstairs noisily. She hoped not to be found and knew that she would be if she didn't move.

There were footsteps on the stairs and then outside the bathroom door. She could hear the doorknob jiggle and the footsteps walk away. Sounds from adjacent rooms implied they had begun to search the upstairs and would soon return to her when they didn't find her in one of the bedrooms.

She listened for gunfire and shouting, anything to determine whether this group was working for her father or not. The police sirens outside had gone quiet, leaving just the flashing of their lights beaming in from around the front of the house. Grace couldn't tell if they were real police cars, the window was faced squarely into the backyard with no chance of seeing the front.

Under the sounds of footfalls, the house was still. The downstairs had gone quiet. The mother was no longer weeping from the kitchen as far as she could tell. Grace slipped back into the porcelain tub. Behind the curtain she melted into the large basin, hoping that she would be over looked when the door was finally opened. Wrapping her arms tightly around herself for protection, she closed her eyes and waited for it to all be over.

***

Peters pulled in behind a police cruiser. An ambulance was circling around to back into the driveway. The house was buzzing with life as uniforms and suits charged around the property, all appearing to be in the pursuit of something imminently important.

The flashing lights lit up the street like a scene from a horror film with blues, reds and whites melding to leave a sinister glow leaking hazardously into the neighbouring yards.

Curious neighbours stood at their windows, hiding behind curtains and blinds to remain unseen by the swarm surrounding their neighbours' home. Lamp posts dotted the street dimly echoing off into the flashing light. They remained unlit, another abnormality in the strange desolate town.

The house sat at the end of a dead end street. It backed straight onto the forest with a steep cliff peering down behind the fence of the backyard. It was a small home. Old and dated, it looked like it had once been a cottage tucked into the trees, until they had been chopped down and new houses had sprung up on demand. The driveway was long, making the home secluded from its fashionable neighbours. It hid behind two large pine trees, needleless and dying. They looked as emancipated as the house itself.

Peters walked in the front door with Platt and King close behind.

Flashing his credentials to the officer at the door, he asked him, "Anything yet?"

"No sir, someone was here, not sure if the girl still is or not."

"Where are my men?"

"Checking the upstairs Sir."

Walking through the gaping hole where the front door had finally fallen off of its hinges. Platt turned to the staircase at the back of the house, marching up two steps at a time. If Grace was still there, she was surely going to distrust him or any other agent or officer that approached her. He looked back at King, waving him to follow. Having met King briefly might be just what they needed to get her to come out of hiding in the tiny house, if she was there at all.

***

Jay was angry when he saw the agents entering the house. Their timing was quicker than he had anticipated. It had thrown a wildcard into the mix. He was going to have to rethink the capture mission entirely before sending his team back in.

He comprised a quick plan, hoping that his team wouldn't see through his daring and into the danger that the plan was going to present them with. He signaled to his men to meet him low on the other side of the hill where they wouldn't be seen.

Men slipped from behind the trees with the whirling of the lights like shadows slipping back into the woods. They moved with such sure feet that they seemed to be only a figment of the imagination, illusions wandering through the night. They slowly approached Jay on the other side quietly freezing as they waited for his command. As the last of the men had gathered around he waved his hand at the ground.

"We are going in... again." He whispered as the men knelt in the dirt around him, "Take her by force. Kill anyone that gets in the way." He kept it short and simple, leaving little room for questions or error. He had worked with these men for fifteen years. They had an understanding and he was going to be very sorry when he lost them.

"Yes Sir." The men mumbled into the night like a small rumble of thunder.

"Through the back and fan out. She is still in there if they're looking."

Jay and his team of eight disappeared into the trees back towards the house. They slipped over the fence unnoticed and silent, pounding through the back door like they were storming a castle.

***

Grace heard more steps on the stairs, followed by mumbling on the other side of the door. The knob began to jiggle intensely as the door shook in its frame. With a click, it gave way falling with a clatter to the bathroom floor. The knob rolled across the floor tapping against the porcelain as it finally settled into a stop.

Grace held her breath, freezing in an awkward position to avoid making any sounds. The door swung open flooding in light from the hallway. Grace cowered in the tub as the light filtered through the curtain blinding her momentarily. She slowly blinked to clear her eyes.

"Grace?" A familiar voice whispered. She tried to place it. It sounded like agent King.

She peeked out around the curtain to see King behind two men in the bathroom door. He slipped through the men and into the bathroom as Grace stood slowly and awkwardly in the bathtub clinging to the curtain. Joy passed over her face as she realized Ethan would be close by.

"King." She gasped with joy as she climbed from the bathtub racing to his side. "Where is Ethan? Is he okay? Are you okay? Were you at the diner when it blew up?" She babbled quietly looking at King, intently waiting for his answers.

"Yes, yes, and yes." He chuckled back with a quiet smile. He was glad to see that she was alright and even more pleased to see her enthusiasm returning.

"Father sent men here to get me, they *are* still here." The words spilled out urgently as she looked over their shoulders and back out the bathroom door. The hall light glowed with the flicker of a bulb that was soon to burn out. "Is your partner okay?" She continued softly, looking into King's eyes guiltily.

"We found him." He nodded sadly, glad that she cared.

A loud bang came from the down the stairs. Gunfire rained from below while more smoke clouded into the air. Shouting sounded loudly as the confusion had had its moment; they had returned.

"How many of them are there?" King asked Grace as he stepped between her and the door.

"I don't know, ten maybe." She stepped back into the bathtub cautiously, "They used smoke last time too." She whispered as smoke rose from the kitchen below. She listened to the shouting beneath them, hoping not to hear Ethan's voice in the crowd. Where was he if not there next to King? She distractedly glanced around looking.

King crossed the room to check the window for an alternate escape route. Through the tempered glass he could see that the drop was too steep to jump. They were going to have to take Grace back through the house to get her out unless they could find a way to get through the window safely.

A mattress wouldn't fit and there wasn't enough time to call a team around the back to catch them in a sheet. The noises coming from the downstairs were chaotic. Getting her down the stairs and through the small full house was out of the question.

King ripped at the window pulling it as far open as he could before it held fast. He ripped the screen off tossing it into the bathtub with a resounding clang through the silent bathroom. The other two men seemed to catch on to King's overall plan. They began searching for anything that might help him in his conquest of the bathroom window. King pulled on the curtain rod; it sprung from the wall cracking the tiles around it. He shook his head and tried the base of the porcelain sink; tugging at it until he was satisfied that it wasn't going anywhere. He looked back to Grace, sizing her up.

"Call more backup in. Let them know there are ten rogue men in the house." Demanded one of the men that had come in with King. He was a short square man of a very solid build he looked up, talking to the taller man at the door beside him.

King looked at her confused expression as she watched them talking. "Grace, these are Platt and Peters, trust them."

Grace looked from a tall Platt to the short stocky Peters. King appeared to believe these men were on their side. He had also believed that the others were. Grace decided to stay as close to King as possible, casting weary glances to his companions.

"Where is Ethan?" She asked, craning her neck to see past the men and into the smoky hallway, still listening for him in the commotion below.

Downstairs she could hear breaking glass as cups and plates were being thrown into the mix. They were trying to conserve their ammunition supplies by fighting with anything around them. A chair was swung, cracking in half as one of the legs spiralled onto the landing outside the bathroom door.

The chaos was getting closer and soon the bathroom would be taken over by the savages downstairs. Grace backed farther into the bathroom waiting for her answer. She wondered if King had heard her, or if he was afraid to tell her the answer.

"In the car." Platt answered flatly.

Grace breathed out with relief, realizing that she had been holding her breath in fear. She looked over to Platt sizing him up for a second time. He seemed alright. She was still going to keep her distance until she knew Ethan was safe for sure.

Until she saw him with her own eyes, she couldn't be sure that this wasn't one of her father's ploys to lure her in. She relaxed her shoulders for a moment before tensing back up at the atrocious sounds from downstairs.

Gunshots were getting closer. They could hear them at their feet as bullets rebounded off of furniture and into the ceiling below their feet. It was becoming very dangerous to stand still. As a bullet pierced through the floor clanging into the side of the sink, they all burst forth in a fury of movement. Their escape was becoming more important as the fight became more intense. Several men were fighting in the kitchen. The agents upstairs were in the hall guarding the stairs.

"King." Grace whispered, pulling him in close so the others wouldn't overhear her. "The files are in Ethan's house."

King looked to Grace startled. He had been curious what the end game had been with convicting Hart. He smiled. "Show me when we get out of this, okay?" Grace nodded in agreement.

***

Downstairs Jay and his team had set off two more smoke grenades in the kitchen and foyer, taking down as many men as they could under the cloud of confusion.

Two of his commandos had snuck out the front to patrol the property, ensuring no one escaped. They monitored the number of cops and agents that went in and out, keeping the perimeter clear. The smoke was slowly dissipating and by the grunts and bangs he could tell they were low on ammo.

Picking up a discarded gun, Jay walked through a small living room searching for the hidden girl. He kicked at low surfaces listening for sounds with his gun pointed forward. He tossed furniture out of his way with a swipe of his boot. The room hadn't left him many places to look, and it was the last room on the main floor of the tiny house.

Now that they had cleared the ground floor they were going to have to separate. Three would go upstairs and three down to the basement; one lay dead on the kitchen floor. Looking up from the bottom of the stairs through the little smoke left, they could see that it was heavily guarded.

Jay smiled. She was probably trapped up there. He sent his team ahead to the upstairs, slinking out back into the yard to wait.

He knew they were outnumbered, his team would thin them out and then he would be waiting, ready to out maneuver them and get the girl back when they left the property with her. Lulling them into a false sense of security was his specialty. It was almost too bad he would have to lose his team over it. He would be sure that the girl paid for it in spades before he turned her over to Hart.

Jay snuck around the side of the property to peek around the front, seeing how his two men were holding up. It was pertinent to his plan that they not die prematurely or she would sneak past him unscathed. He could tell from their dark jackets that they were hiding beside a car, guns ready and near enough to take out any opposition entering or exiting the home.

He was almost proud of them for a moment before he snuck back into the trees to watch from a distance. Close enough to see what was going on and far enough to get to his car if this invoked a pursuit.

***

Ethan sat in the back of the car, hunched so as not to be seen by the two armed men outside the car. He folded himself into the space at his feet, keeping them in view. The tips of their weapons popped up into sight through the window momentarily. He held his breath afraid he had been spotted.

They didn't look like the good guys and they were heavy with guns and strings of bullets. He held his breath for a moment longer as the guns receded back out of sight. More likely they were settling themselves in for a long wait, watching the house from under the car and through the many cars mirrors.

They had a good vantage point and would be able to see anything happening in or around the small house. Ethan was stuck there. He slid down further into the alcove behind the driver seat.

He reached under the front seat, searching for anything that might help if the men saw him. He felt a cylinder. Pulling from under the seat, he saw that it was a road flare.

It would have to do.

He clutched it tight, silently watching the armed men duck beside his window after standing to check the houses' door. Breathing slowly, so as not to be overheard by the close by gunmen, Ethan slowly twisted his body so he could see out one of the side mirrors without being seen through the window. The position was uncomfortable, but at least he could see the front of the house and maybe warn someone before retaliating gunfire pelted him through the car. He waited silently, breathing shallowly through the pain in his ribcage.

From the car, Ethan could hear the gunfire in the house. He watched the smoke pouring out of the hollow of the front door into the red and blue flashing lights of the night. Ethan thought the house had been set on fire and couldn't imagine why there was so much fighting happening over one girl.

It must be Grace in there; he thought hopefully wishing she could come through the doors soon. But not before the rouge gunmen were taken out.

He could hear glass shattering and watched as the outside of the house slowly started to resemble what he imagined the inside was looking like.

Shutters fell from window frames and glass from the windows themselves as bullets pierced every inch of the house ripping it apart from the inside out. He could tell that the previously curious neighbours had all closed their blinds to the implosion of the house at the end of the street.

They would likely be cowering in their basements until morning, clinging to baseball bats and garden shears for protection. The thought made him sick. People were willing to watch others suffer. Unless it could get them hurt, then they would cower away never offering up a helping hand.

***

Men had approached the bottom of the stairs, King ordered the agents to shoot and keep them in the downstairs. They treated the upstairs like their fortress, guarding the only entrance with a vigilant hand. The extra men stood guard behind their counterparts creating a second blockade. They held their guns at the ready.

Gunfire broke out in a haze of slow moving smoke and debris fell as the house began tearing apart. Bullets pelted thought the drywall, leaving smoking holes of dust fluttering into the madness.

Grace ducked, fearful of bullets whizzing past the lines of men between her and the stairs. A fire had broken out in the kitchen, the smoke wafting in to replace the thick smoulder of the grenades that had all but thinned out into nothing.

The fire alarms had gone berserk, melding with the police sirens into a melancholy song. King and his counterparts were rushing around her, heads ducked to the falling debris. She had no idea what they were doing. All she could do was watch as the ceiling outside of the bathroom began falling in pieces.

The hall light had finally lost its flicker, going out completely. She wasn't sure if it was due to the old bulb or the barrage of gunfire. It was obvious that the men at the bottom of the stairs had doubled their numbers. They knew she was up there from the barricade of officers guarding the stairs. She watched through the dark hall as the fire crept up higher, black smoke billowing towards her like the breath of a fire-breathing dragon threatening to roast her if she didn't leave soon.

Behind her the glass of the window shattered. King was beating at the leftover shards with the toilet seat and then covering the sill with a thick folded towel. She looked back out the door closing her ears to all the yelling and sirens and gunfire, they were ringing from the strain. Grace felt as if she were in a horrific nightmare.

The shock of it all was causing her to see it all in clips and pieces; smoke, fire, window, rope. She didn't know how, but she was suddenly standing outside looking at a black car.

Out of the back window a flare went off, Grace ducked. Gunfire sounded. She looked up to see Ethan's face, smiling and then she fainted.

MARKED

The smoke was billowing up the stairs, black and thick consuming the hallway in swirls that grew lower and lower. They ducked under the heaviest parts avoiding the inevitable breath of burning smoke entering their lungs.

King pulled Grace in as the flames began flickering within view, pulling her away from the door where she stood like a statue frozen in the encroaching heat. Platt had rummaged through a hallway closet, passing folded piles to his partner as Peters tied the pile of sheets into a rope. He wrapped it around Grace and King.

They ducked out the window as the rope was tied off, propelling lazily into the backyard. King kept one hand around Grace holding the sheet-rope steady as his other hand held his pistol steady with his sweeping eyes as they lowered to the ground.

Peters and Platt were followed out by two of their men moments later landing softly on the patchy grass. King untied himself and Grace as they stood point. A fire crew was already hooking up their hose out front when they slipped around the side into view of the car waiting. Having been on route to the initial call they were not wasting time to take out the cause of the smoke.

King turned to his car as a flare erupted out the back window. He pulled his gun just in time to meet the two strangers as they leapt from behind the vehicle, caught off guard by the sudden lightshow.

He fired twice.

They slowly hit the stone walkway, dead.

Around the corner of the house the rest of their men had climbed down the rope and were filing through the yard, cautious of falling debris and smoke. They were coughing from the putrid air of the bathroom they had come from.

One of them had set the rope on fire hoping to deter the others from following. It sent up spirals of light smoke into the flashing air. Peters was down behind him with Platt holding him up. He had been shot in the left leg as the last man had fallen, pulling the trigger as he dropped.

Platt helped him hobble over to the closest emergency vehicle, a fire truck, to sit him down. Paramedics approached cautiously searching for other threats while Ethan raced from the car. He held Grace's face in his hands. She smiled as her eyes rolled back in her head.

Peters winced as the paramedic cleaned his wound, snarling at the house like it had wounded him personally. He bit back sour words as he was bandaged up, testing his leg while popping back some pain medication handed to him with a bottle of water. The paramedic team scooted off looking for more injured, cowering from every loud noise like scared animals during hunting season.

"I'm taking them out of here." King told Platt as he lifted Grace from the walkway. He began marching towards the first shiny black vehicle parked just past the emergency crew.

Ethan was quick in tow as he walked to the car. King set Grace to the ground where Ethan took over holding her steady. He looked under the visor on the driver side, producing a set of keys. Turning them into the ignition he sat in the seat as the engine turned over. King stepped out to pick up Grace and slide her into the back seat. Ethan climbed in with her, settling her head on his lap and brushing the hair from her face. King looked over to Peters, sitting in his own bullet riddled car behind him.

Peters had taken up the driver seat, despite his injured leg and was revving his engine at King in acknowledgement.

They were going too.

Platt slipped in to the passenger seat as a second set of men walked off to find their own car to trail with. It looked like they were getting an entourage after all.

"What's your address." King looked back at Ethan, giving the other set of men time to find a car in the mess behind them.

"What? You're not taking us to my house. She needs to be somewhere safe." Ethan protested.

"She said there is a file there and we need it to get this case closed." King turned, looking Ethan in the eyes over the back of his seat, "Before Hart burns them to the ground too." He added very seriously, turning to the house to make his point.

"It's the mansion on Mill Creek." Ethan concluded. He held Grace close to warm her. "Two fifty-seven." He added, talking to the back of King's head.

"We pick the files up, and take her back to a safe house. Others will be there." King assured Ethan, seeing the look of horror passing over his tired grungy face.

Ethan gritted his teeth, knowing that he couldn't talk King out of it. He was right about Hart; he would likely try to burn the manor down next hoping to put an end to their source once and for all. Hart didn't know where Grace had kept the files but he surely suspected the manor, as he had already tried to burn it down once before.

King stepped out of the car momentarily. Walking to the two idling cars behind him, he told them of his plans to take Ethan and Grace back to a mansion on Mill Creek in Monticello. Giving them the address for their GPS devices they nodded out their windows, staying in an idle until King took the lead with Grace and Ethan in his car.

King pulled a radio from Peters' car radioing the tech team that they were splitting and their new destination. When King climbed back in behind the wheel, he entered a number into the GPS and set them into drive.

"Are you going to be okay?" He asked Ethan slowly, looking at him in the rear view mirror. The reflecting lights gave him a sallow pale look like that of the seasick about to heave overboard.

"Yes." Ethan whispered, hoping he was right. King started rolling forward slowly giving Ethan a moment to collect himself. He didn't want to be dealing with vomit on top of everything else.

***

Peters had been shot in the leg. It had grazed his inner thigh leaving him with a wad of cotton wrapped over with gauze. He looked ridiculous and felt even worse. The sting of the bullet wound was worsened by the burn around the edges where the heat of the bullet had cauterized part of the wound.

It was nothing fatal and the paramedics were already done fixing him up. He wasn't about to wait around for their second opinion. Peters was filled with adrenaline from the graze and was ready to drive. He just hoped King could keep up. He got the feeling it was going to be a quick drive.

Platt sat quietly in the passenger seat punching in numbers and holding a phone to his ear as he waited on hold with a technical crew. He was always so serious and down to earth. He worked well with the chaotic spunk of Peters, mellowing him out enough to keep him sharp.

"Follow King." Peters suggested seeing the fight in his partners weary face growing as the chase resumed. "I'll get the address entered in here, just keep him in sight."

Platt didn't look up from his devices as Peters shot forward into the empty street ahead, playing chicken with the driver of the third car as they exited the subdivision.

Platt nodded smiling widely, "Take it easy bud." He looked out to the third vehicle, giving the driver a look of reprimand that caused them to fall in line behind him quickly.

Glancing back momentarily at the burning building in his wake Peters hit the gas and sped off after King. Plowing over a speed bump, he sent Platt grasping for his fallen devises and his seatbelt all at once while sending up glances of loathing over his shoulder at the speed demon behind the wheel driving. Peters grinned like a maniac peering into the windshield like he was back in a racing game and going for an achievement.

***

Hart was not a patient man. He called Jay to check his progress with no answer. He didn't often tolerate a missed call, but he understood that Jay's timing was precious in a dive and dash like this.

Trying to get Grace away from that house before the police arrived was going to be hard enough without her inevitable retaliation. Now that she had tasted freedom she had developed an insatiable thirst for it and had been fighting his advances tooth and nail to stay in the open air.

Switching his phone to the GPS tracker he saw that the two cars were heading back to Monticello. Satisfied that they must be on route with Grace, he let it slide that Jay hadn't answered his call; she was likely putting up a fight as they tried to sedate her.

He chose to give them thirty more minutes, after that heads would roll. He was running out of resources and if his daughter was let free she had enough information to incarcerate him and most of his employees for the rest of their lives.

He had pulled all the strings he had available to him to facilitate her capture, it was the highest priority at the moment. Business partners were calling him on his other phone every five minutes demanding progress as they heard of the church fire over the media.

News was spreading like wildfire, he had already given his business phone to one of the lackeys here at the holding cells to take his calls and advise the others that matters were still in Hart's control.

He could feel it spiraling away from him minute by minute. The longer she was out, the more evidence she left trailing along behind her of her own identity.

The fact that she was even still alive was enough to take him down in court. Having faked his daughter's death ten years ago was surely a federal offence.

He spoke loudly across the quiet building, "I hope you are all learning from these foolish mistakes. I will not tolerate *failure*." He hissed.

The guards sat straight in their chairs and began to look busy, fearful that he would take his displeasure out on them again. They jumped at every huff or flinch as he sat in a chair watching the tiny television set he had playing the local news. He watched as it recapped the freak fires at the church and cabin and frowned as a new story was breaking in the town of Oneida.

That was where Jay and his team were coming from; he leaned in and turned the volume up with a furious curiosity as his work phone began buzzing with more intensity across the room.

***

Jay crept out through the busy backyard, avoiding stares from paramedics and fire fighters. He stayed low under the smoke screen. No one could see him as he slipped away into the night. He mounted the fence cautiously slipping over the side yard into the neighbouring backyard.

He raced through connecting yards. Dashing over fences and through hedges with no regard for maintaining the properties integrity, he damaged fence after fence until he was clear of the confusion and able to return to the main streets.

News crews were jostling down the less crowded streets trying to capture images of the spiraling smoke flashing blue and red from the patrol vehicles lighting up in its proximity, without getting too close to the gunfire and danger.

Jay avoided them cautiously taking two extra backyards to get past their tyrannical rants, all sounding so proper while the cameras were flashing and then whipping out the profanities as the light stopped flashing and ashes started falling on their perfect hair.

He certainly didn't envy them in their dull listless lives. Backtracking two streets over to where he had left the second vehicle, he threw himself onto the driver's seat, not wanting to waste time catching up.

Once behind the wheel, Jay snapped down a screen on the console. Both of their vehicles had been equipped with GPS trackers and the other blip was moving away down the road back to Monticello. One of the agents was driving the other car and with luck he could trail them easily until a chance came up to overpower and conquer. Jay started his engine and whipped it into drive. His life depended on retrieving the girl, dead or alive. And he was not about to give up now.

Blood pooled from a wound on his leg. He let up on the gas momentarily to twist a tourniquet of material around to staunch the bleeding, swerving for a second over the curb beside him. Then with a quick whip of his head to look behind him, he sped forward with a velocity that would normally win him first place in the street races he loved.

RISKY

Grace had regained consciousness shortly after King had whipped the car into drive. Disoriented at first, Ethan had explained quickly where they were going. She didn't protest, looking to the back of King's head knowingly.

Once the files were retrieved she would be useless and maybe her father would leave her alone. Or maybe he would kill her anyway, no need to keep her alive if he was going to jail for the rest of his life anyway. She pushed the thought away trying to remember the details in the files and why they were so important after all these years. She hoped they were still intact, tucked away in her secret hiding spot.

King had been driving for ten minutes while the two whispered in the back seat, staying close so he wouldn't overhear. Ethan held Grace's hand, pulling her closer they were cheek to cheek when she shared her secret with him.

"I left the files in the spare room." She whispered into his ear, like a pirate telling of a treasure trove. He pulled back looking into her eyes curiously.

"I searched every inch of the house." He shook his head confused.

"Your dad even tried to burn it down once…" He chuckled. "I never found anything." He blinked as though he were clearing his head. "Not even in the secret cupboard."

"There was a loose floorboard in the closet, behind that secret wall." She admitted, lowering her eyes.

Grace and Ethan had found the secret sliding wall in the spare rooms closet when they were very young. They had often snuck treats upstairs and after the kitchen was locked up for the night they would huddle together in the closet sitting on pillows eating their secret treasure.

"Seriously? I checked that spot." His face lit up with excitement, momentarily thrilled about the new hiding place. "I didn't know about the floorboard though. Why didn't you tell me?" His brow furrowed with worry that maybe Grace hadn't trusted him before her kidnapping. Or that they had ended things on bad terms in her mind.

"I didn't have time." Grace smiled. "I'm glad you found me."

"Me too." Ethan whispered.

Grace was resting her head on Ethan's shoulder. She wrapped her fingers into his and whispered into his ear. "I was going to climb out of the tower and get to you. I had a rope and everything…"

Ethan laughed. The sound was wonderful to Grace's ears.

King cut in. "Shit." He was looking into the side mirrors confused.

Grace and Ethan sat up straight. Grace looked behind her out of the back window. A car was weaving through the single line of traffic, pushing cars off the road into the narrow ditch beside the forest.

Headlights were weaving in and out of cars, flashing high beams at them through their back windows. Something was amiss in the cavalcade behind them.

King sped up slightly as a precaution; the car in front of him seemed to have the same idea, racing for the next off-ramp.

Two cars behind them, their backup agents swerved into the oncoming lane to avoid a collision.

The renegade car was getting closer, taking the opportunity to almost pass them. They veered back in, cutting the car off just in time to send him slamming his brakes in the now vacant oncoming lane. Cars piled up behind the agents giving them some room before the rebel found an opening back in.

King hit the gas, Grace and Ethan jolted into the back of the seat as the car accelerated. Ahead, the road was splitting into two lanes. King drove up the bumper of the car in front of him, honking his horn to entice it into acceleration.

"We have to lose them before we get to the house." King yelled over the revving of the engines and the chaos of the crashed cars behind them.

Horns were honking and cars were veering madly trying to escape the wrath of the rouge car as it jolted through traffic, a knight in pursuit of a king.

***

Jay was glad he had taken his own ride in for the job. Hiding it a block away had led suspicion only to the lowly black Charger they were currently commandeering ahead of him.

It had been purchased by Hart and left in the lot to be taken on special cases; something that looked federal. It was often used for easy captures of professionals or higher end targets, the cases where the typical black van might look suspicious.

In fact they tried to steer clear of that stereotype altogether. It was a bad reputation to have and Hart deemed them much classier than that. The Charger had some speed to it, but it worked like a snail compared to his Camero. With all the specs and even a few illegal upgrades courtesy of Hart, he was nearly unbeatable. Things that made his car a write-off, if you could write-off a kidnapping vehicle that is.

It was suitable for any job, most of them dirty and under the table; just the way Jay liked to do business. The car was a perk for taking the position of head recruiter. He handpicked most of the men Hart and his associates used for their dirtier jobs. He had an eye for loyal thugs.

Jay ran his hand across the dashboard as the car purred, switching into a higher gear. "Time to test out the new specs." He scowled.

Flashing the high beams ahead of him, he hoped to confuse the traffic enough to distract from his next move. He swerved out and then back taking a glance at the car ahead, it was close.

At least two cars followed behind it, sleek and black they had set themselves firmly between him and his target. He had to get them off the road if he hoped to get the girl alone.

Jay was pissed. He could see them ahead but the road was only one lane and traffic was moving too slowly. He jumped into the oncoming lane and plunged back into the car beside him, toppling it off the road. He revved his engine at the next car, bumping against the back end, willing it to give up and surrender to the shoulder of the road and allow him to pass.

Brake lights flashed at him in response. He whipped back into the oncoming lane and tipped back knocking that car to the side of the road too. Patience was not his strongest suit and he could see his target only a few lengths ahead of him.

He revved up again looking expectantly to the next obstacle in his way; the minivan swerved trying to hit the shoulder of the road without slowing down. Jay grinned; at least they were starting to get it.

The night was cool, he had the sunroof open a crack, bringing in fresh air and keeping him sharp after a long day. The oncoming traffic was arriving wearily in a clump obviously nervous of passing the insanity of their opposing lane; seeing smoke and crashed cars ahead of them they could only guess at what was happening.

The car with the GPS tag was honking its horn trying to get ahead in traffic. Jay had to catch up before the lanes split into two, it would be more difficult to block two lanes and force them into a standoff.

He revved up, scraping the side of the van as he passed it by. It toppled in a spiral downwards into the trees, the breaking glass barely registered above the honking and revving of engines. Oncoming cars swerved outwards as they passed, giving him room. He grinned maniacally gritting his teeth as he locked in on his target. He saw movement in the back of the GPS tagged car. She was in there for sure; it would be easier than he had hoped.

***

"Watch out!" Grace screamed as a transport entered the highways on-ramp, oblivious to the traffic confusion beside it. The truck slowly merged over as King swerved.

The lanes split to two just in time. He could see the transport brush by, barely missing his mirror by an inch. Cars behind them were swerving to hit the next exit ramp, not willing to be involved in the car chase building up on the road.

It left the highway nearly clear for their pursuer to catch up. King looked nervous as his buffer of cars slowly vanished, barely being replaced by one or two coming onto the on-ramp still between them. Tossing a phone over his shoulder he yelled back to Ethan urgently.

"Press three and hold it, ask for Platt. They will patch you through."

Ethan picked up the phone and frantically pressed at the screen trying to get the button to work. Finally it clicked and began to ring. He covered one ear and pressed the phone up to the other.

Cars ahead were separating into the two lanes, disregarding the chaos behind them. King swerved again, propelling them a few more car lengths away from the pursuer behind them. He was glad for the unaware cars that had entered after the piles of cars had been tossed into the ditch. They still drove on oblivious to the psycho coming up behind them, and even gave King a hard time trying to pass them putting more space between his car and the crazed car torpedoing towards them.

"What's the cars tag number?" Ethan asked loudly, phone pressed to his ear. King furrowed his brow as he searched frantically across the dash board while checking his mirrors for openings to plow into.

The car swerved back to the second lane. "There isn't one." His voice was verging on hysterical. He looked back, catching his cool before Grace or Ethan could see him. "There isn't one." He repeated with more patience, firmly gritting his teeth.

It was then that King realized it was not one of their cars. The man in pursuit of them probably had the car tagged and if they were really lucky he *didn't* have it rigged with explosives as well. King searched with one hand for anything under the seat as he continued to swerve thorough traffic.

Peters would be proud of him for some of the manoeuvres he had pulled; when this was over he was challenging him to a race. King sat back up straight as he gave up on trying to find a bomb under his seat, either way he was dead if he didn't get away from that car.

He looked in the mirrors to see where it was. It was getting closer and ahead cars obstructed his way.

***

Peters was in a rage, sticking close behind King, he radioed the other agents to hold up a blockade with him as the highway split to two lanes.

Preventing the crazed car from catching up to King as he wove on ahead of them was essential. Platt was on the phone with Ethan. "That's not a federal car." He turned to Peters,

"Tell them to check for a tracker." Peters answered as they were rear ended jolting them forward.

He gritted his teeth and flashed a finger towards the back of the car. Not that it mattered, he knew they wouldn't see it in the dark, but it made him feel slightly better and vented some of his rage.

"We're going to have to switch them out of that car." Platt answered after a muffled chat with Ethan on the other end.

"Gotta lose this guy first." Peters answered.

Braking and pulling back, he looped around their target catching him on the line divider between himself and the other ford SUV. Together they closed in, metal scraped, sparks flew. The deep red Camero tried to shoot forward and was caught by the SUVs cramming in closer.

Brake lights glowed from the back, as it slipped out from between them. Taking a page out of Peters' book it whipped back, sending the two SUVs sailing towards one another. They quickly pulled back into position.

This guy was good.

Platt stayed on the phone while Peters searched his mirrors for the Camero. The night was dark and starting to cloud over, only the lights of the other cars lit up the road. Most of the cars were slowing down to pull over, smart enough to see the chase running up behind them. Peters frowned as less traffic left him less opportunity to block King from being caught and rammed off the road into a tree.

***

Jay fell back, pulling in behind a transport. He judged the far shoulder to be wide enough for the pass. Slipping up the far side of the transport, he whipped back in unannounced, colliding with the two SUVs and pushing them into the oncoming lane of traffic over the median.

Sparks flew up as they pushed back nearly sending Jay tumbling down the hill beside the soft shoulder. He pushed the car into a higher gear and shot forward ahead of them.

ESCAPE

Finally gaining ground on his intended target he looked over to the closer SUV as he passed. He didn't recognize the two suited agents in the front. That meant she was defiantly up front in his other car.

He locked sight with the black Charger ahead, still weaving through the thinning traffic. Jay knew the car didn't have as much power as his and as soon as the traffic cleared he could take them out easily. Getting rid of the two goons on his tail was another matter entirely.

The SUVs were revving up behind him. The one in the left lane had pulled a gun out the passenger window. Jay alternated accelerating and coasting to disrupt their aim as gunfire pelted at the pavement, aimed for his tires.

Jay twisted the wheel plowing into the front of the firing SUV. Its companion surprisingly shot up beside him, keeping him close to the guardrail. He was wedged in with nowhere to fallback. Jay smiled evilly.

DANGEROUS

King could see out the rear view that traffic was thinning out. Hitting the gas even harder, he barely noticed a difference in speed.

They had reached maximum velocity. The dashboard lit red and was flashing at him, willing him to slow before the engine blew out. He pressed on, whipping around a startled truck. The swerving caused a small three wheeler it had stowed on the flatbed to roll onto the highway, crashing into a million pieces as it impacted with the asphalt. The commotion sent cars veering for the side of the road in a more panicked frenzy than before.

Grace was clutching the headrest with white knuckles staring out the back window, reiterating the movement of the cars behind her to alleviate some of the stress behind King's racing eyes.

Her face was pale and panicked. She still wore the filthy coat Chung had given to her, it hung wet and large on her small frame. To a passing car she might look like an excited kid staring out the back window of her parent's car on a family trip.

Ethan clutched the phone close to his ear. Although still on the line with Platt, neither had spoken a word in minutes. Heavy breathing and gasps as the cars shook were the only transmissions passing through the receivers. Sweat clung to Ethan's sallow face; giving him the look of a fevered addict, shaking in the seat while staring into nothingness. He was lost in the panic and unable to function with any efficiency.

***

Platt sprung back to life as Peters shouted. "Cut off ahead. Tell King to go right."

Putting the phone harder to his ear he yelled at the receiver. "Ethan, Ethan..." After waiting a moment for a response he continued on. "Tell King stay right, tell King stay right."

Ahead he could see King switching lanes for the cut off. They would be safe for a while, at least long enough to ditch the tracked car; if Peters and his backup man could keep the Camero veering into the left that is.

Peters held the wheel firm, matching the pattern of acceleration and coasting. The car appeared like a bucking bronco trailing down the highway within a cage of SUVs trying to maneuver its way out and off to snatch its prey.

The cut off was fast approaching and the Camero was veering towards Peters, trying to cut across into the right lane. It sped forward shooting out of the SUV's primitive cage like a horse starting a race.

Peters stepped on the gas, cutting him off. He clipped the side of the car, sending it on an awkward turn as it pulled back into position between him and the guardrail.

Pieces of his mirror rained backwards across his windshield, twinkling like rubies in the red lights of the bumper ahead of them. Peters squinted through the glittering shower turning his head to catch sight of the car that was now lingering in his gaping blind spot.

The car swerved again, trying to catch Peters off guard. He held fast sending a swirl of sparks into the night air. The side mirror shattered sending a crack right across the front windshield of the fancy car as it went flying back into the rear SUV.

The road was splitting and with one last veer, the Camero shot forward making a break for the separating lane. Peters didn't miss a beat, punching forward and slamming it in the back right of the bumper he sent it spinning backwards until it was facing him dead on.

Peters looked into the driver's eyes for a split second before the impact sent him back over the median and rolling into oncoming traffic.

Shattered glass and debris rained down behind them as they slowed to the side of the road. Flipping on a set of integrated red and blues they backed up along the shoulder until they made it to the cut off they had passed.

Peters and Platt remained still for an extra moment, making sure the car was done rolling on the other side of the guardrail. Smoke wafted in a snakelike trail from the engine of the crumpled car, a tire rolled lazily down the shoulder.

Traffic continued to move slowly past the scene. With everyone wanting a look at the wreckage, but no one was willing to stop and help the stranger in the dark of night.

The two vehicles switched over to the right exit that King had taken and drove on to meet him.

***

King had pulled to the side of the road a few miles into the cut off. Cars were starting to resume their pace now that the swerving cars had disappeared taking the chase with them onto the other ramp. The late night air was cool and the clouds had cleared leaving the heavens visible above.

King stood at the trunk of the car, letting Ethan and Grace stand further onto the shoulder, sheltered from oncoming cars by the burnt out Charger. They watched with anticipation and looked ready to pounce at a moment's notice.

Grace's eyes darted between the line of trees and the road. She looked ready to take off into the trees again if things went south. Welts lined the doors of the car where they had scraped against passing vehicles.

King stretched out, cautious with his neck as he reached a hand up to massage his shoulders while he waited, curious of how he was going to feel in the morning when all of his muscles finally tensed back up. The night was still asides from the zoom of the passing cars.

King could hear the impact of the cars hitting across the highway beyond the thin tree filled median that separated them from the other roadway where they had split.

Scraping metal and splashing debris hitting the pavement made more loud noises. With a final loud crunch, the road returned to a normal highway filled with the sounds of speeding cars. A transport passed whipping wind into his face. It sounded like the chase was finally over. He watched in the distance as the flashing blue and red of the mangled SUVs reached them from around a bend.

Pulling to the side, Platt called from a broken window. "Hop in."

King chuckled, unable to wrench the back door open he lifted Grace up into the backseat through the broken window allowing Ethan to follow before climbing in himself.

They sped off into the night, feeling like action heroes.

***

Hart watched his phone curiously as the first blip disappeared and the second pulled to the side of the road five miles from the old Evans estate and stopped.

Why on Earth would they be taking Grace that direction unless they were chasing another car with her in it? That pile of rot wasn't even on his manifesto. None of his men knew where the Evans' lived anymore. Hart thought for a moment; unless it wasn't his men driving.

Grace was retrieving the files.

He knew that house should have burned to the ground years ago. He turned to the closest security guard. "Pull your car around front." He ordered stiffly, "We're going for a drive."

The guard nodded and took off for the parking lot at a jog.

Hart sneered, these thugs were so dependable and at the same time so disposable and useless. Back in the day he only needed one go to man, one man who would get the job done or die trying. Now everyone was so familiar with outsourcing it was hard to find good help.

Hart pondered for a moment while he waited. Grace was beyond hope at this point. The FBI had had their hooks in her for too long. She had become disposable and he was keenly aware that this was going to be his responsibility.

After years of keeping her safe and locked away he was finally going to have to kill his daughter to keep his secrets safe. If his business partners found her first they would surely have less mercy than he. They had just as much hanging in the balance and even if she were to perish now, it had to be with the files readily taken back. Before agents had an opportunity to get their grimy little hands on all of his contacts.

Hart scowled even more, wrinkling his aging face in a contorted manner. He was verging on fury and just as he was about to snap the neck of the technician beside him, the car pulled around the bend into sight. As the car sped towards him the tires screeched to a halt.

Hart stepped around the vehicle to the driver's door, pulling it open he looked to the guard. "I'm driving." He demanded, stepping back briefly as the guard scurried to the passenger side while leaving the car in park.

Hart was furious and it was time to take matters into his own hands, even if he had to burn the house to the ground with Grace in it.

Climbing into the low driver seat, Hart reached under to adjust it, pulling himself forward over the wheel like a man who didn't believe in tomorrow. He switched to drive and pressed his heavy foot to the gas while the guard scrambled to close the side door. They sped into the dark early morning recklessly. Hart flicked the radio to a sports talk show calming the guard by giving the illusion that he was listening for updates on his missed game as he drove.

No point in riling the poor man up just yet. Chances were he would be dead before they ever got back into the car again.

This time he was taking Grace down with him.

***

The SUV turned slowly, rattling under the hood. A back tire had popped a mile back and the wheel well scraped on the ground leaving deep gouges in the pavement as the car rolled forward sparking onto the dark lawn, pulling up the drive towards the mansion.

Grace couldn't help but notice how dilapidated it looked. As the headlights passed over it she could see that singed stone ringed the lower windows, indications of the fire her father had tried to start. The rocks crumbled on the driveway and the lawn left unmaintained resembled patches of field. Tall grass and brambles mingled to create a hazardous path.

Parts of the driveway were cracked and overgrown and the tire well caught, revving the engine up to near maximum before they popped out of the divot with a startling jolt. Grace looked to Ethan her mouth agape as more of the sprawling mansion came in to view.

"What happened?" She asked slowly as her eyes rolled wide in her head, looking over his shoulder in horror.

In fact the house looked like it would fit in just right for Halloween; the gaping holes where the upper windows had once been gave the house a jack-o-lantern look. Like it was waiting to be lit from the inside, rotting like a pumpkin that had been left on the step a week too long.

"I don't live here anymore." He answered simply. A haunted look passed his face as he turned to the mansion before them.

The house had held nothing but bad memories for Ethan after Grace had left. It had been a reminder that he had once had a family and a friend and after his father and Grace had left it had become a hollow place filled with memories that he was not ready to face. Not even the family butler, Jerry, had liked the place after that.

They had moved together and maintained the house from a distance, letting it fall into disrepair after the fire had consumed a whole wing of the second story.

"Not since before the fire, it wasn't the same without you and my dad anyway." Ethan leaned out the broken window of the SUV, looking up at his father's old office window.

It had always glowed with a warm yellow light, late into the night. He had often doubted that the light was ever turned off. After his dad had gone, Ethan left the light on until it had finally burnt out and he had been too afraid to go back in after that. Too many memories of his father that he hadn't been ready to face were hidden behind those doors.

Some nights back in college he would drive by the mansion before going home to the little house he and Jerry had bought, just to see his father's office glowing in the dim lights of dusk. It had been a comfort then, now seeing the hollow place where the window had once gleamed left a gaping hole in his heart. He wished he had gone in there one last time before the fire had consumed it whole.

"I'm sorry..." Grace had almost forgotten that Ethan's father had been killed the day she was kidnapped. She had been dragged into the same van as his bleeding body and was taken with him when they dumped his lifeless corpse.

ESCAPE

Ethan probably didn't even know where his father's body was. He had likely been buried with an empty casket like the one at her funeral. Her father had let her watch the video of her funeral afterwards. Ethan's tears had haunted her for years. He lost his father and his best friend on the same day.

She couldn't imagine the pain he had felt as a thirteen year old boy. She had watched him weep. They had both been buried in the same cemetery a year and a half after their disappearance, neither of the bodies had been found but at that point they had both been presumed dead. In her case it was a well thought out hoax that had left her sitting on a shelf away from her own life for ten years gathering dust.

Ethan's father had not been so lucky.

The car stopped before the massive front steps, decaying and growing weeds in the cracks that lined their previously elegant state. The other vehicle pulled up behind them, idling loudly in the circular drive. The passenger window was missing and a rear view mirror hung uselessly at its side. The spatter of broken glass and debris from the vehicle had left a patchwork of indents along the front, exposing metal under the otherwise shiny black paint. It looked like a firework etched into the front hood.

"Wait." King had instructed as the other men exited their cars and approached.

King climbed out and instructed them to stay on the main level while they were inside; watching for a rescue team that was waiting in reserve and ready to go when they placed the call.

Turning with a wave, Platt tugged on the rear door of the broken vehicle. Kicking against the front door as it finally gave way with a loud pop falling off of its hinges on to the cracked pavement of the round driveway. He escorted Ethan and Grace out through the broken metal and glass of the fallen door and up to the crumbling first step.

Grace took the steps quickly, waiting for them all at the top. Even hidden in shadows her hair shone bright orange like a beacon leading the way. Grace was still wary of the other agent and stayed close beside Ethan and King. Avoiding Platt's concerned stares she watched them wearily from the top of the steps.

Looking out across the moon lit lawn the driveway looked as though it was filled with the aftermath of a derby. Car pieces pinged as they hit the pavement, falling loosely from the vehicles in the light breeze. The night lit up behind them, full of stars on the lightless property. Grace looked up to see the familiar stars huddling over the mayhem of the unmaintained land, it chilled her. She tugged Chung's damp coat closer again wrapping the front edges past themselves until it was tight. She turned back to Ethan who was now atop the front stoop beside her.

Ethan reached for a key hidden under a fake piece of flagstone. It was the only thing on the steps that looked clean. The plastic was slightly melted at the edges, giving it away as a fake. He twisted the key in the lock with a little force and then he pushed the door open after pausing for a long breath of the fresh air outside.

The acrid stench of decay and burnt wood welcomed them to the once immaculate mansion, rolling out like a welcome mat over the front steps. Grace walked in through her memories; reaching for the wall inside the door fumbling in the dark she tried the switch for the lights.

Flipping it expectantly she waited. Looking at her hand in confusion, she tried again, switching it off and then on again. She looked up to the ceiling wondering if the bulbs needed replaced. She tried the next switch before Ethan caught on to what she was doing.

"Sorry, I haven't paid that bill in years." Ethan answered, embarrassed when nothing happened again.

The house that Grace remembered was covered in years of disrepair.

Wallpaper peeled from the walls while water damage from the fire had warped the once shiny hardwood floors. Her breath caught in her throat as she looked to the dark walls, seeing broken pictures melting in their frames filled with shards of broken glass.

In the dim moonlight trailing through the door it looked like she was in hell. To Grace it felt like she really had died. The house reflected all the pain she had felt locked alone in the tower. The only thing she had feared for all those years was not failure to escape or her own death, but that nothing would be there if she ever *did* find her way past the prisons walls.

Emotions welled up within her as she looked from the foyer to the kitchen, gloomy and barely visible in the dim light of the moon shining over her.

She remembered Jerry scolding her for taking too many cookies, always joking and smiling. She remembered whenever her father's maid would drop her off for a particularly long stay she would come in to the kitchen and have tea with Jerry. Grace was always invited to sit with them and it made her feel so welcome and at home.

When this was all over she didn't know where she would go or what she would do. It wasn't something she had ever thought of before now. She had always just focused on the escape itself, not the aftermath or the rest of her life after that. For now Grace just knew she had to get herself free from her father.

King chuckled and pulled a small flashlight from his belt. Flipping a switch it cast a bright blue tinge across the room pulling the damage into sharp relief. Platt clicked a button on his phone, lighting the grand foyer even brighter, above them the chandelier twinkled through the dust, dim and foreboding.

Ethan led them to the stairs taking caution to test each step for rot before Grace had reached it. Several steps gave way under his weight leaving him tugging on the frail railing for support as King and Peters tugged him back out again, carefully stepping over the hole as they kept pace with him. Slowly they made their way to the second floor.

It was even more depressing than the foyer. Grace looked down the hallway, trying to picture it as she remembered. The memories welled up inside her again and a tear escaped and rolled down her cheek onto the rough floor beneath her. It was like seeing her favourite place gutted from the inside out.

The harsh blue lights cast about leaving sharp shadows. It gave Grace the impression of a nightmare. Piles of boxes lined the halls clumsily stacked. Doors sat open leading to rooms she had never been allowed to see. The order was missing and Grace could feel the world spinning beneath her. She reached to Ethan for support, catching a dusty pile of boxes instead. They tumbled to the floor at her feet.

She looked down in a daze, memories spilling forward as though the dam in her mind had finally broken spilling forth the things she had suppressed to survive her incarceration.

Her old trinket box had exploded at her feet, spilling all the silly rocks and beads she and Ethan had collected in the woods behind the house. She stared at the scattered pile mesmerised. She had forgotten all the little things that had kept them busy, running around the mansion like children on a pirate adventure or a dinosaur expedition. They had roamed this house like it was a playground, racing the halls for pleasure.

She understood now why most of the doors were kept closed. Not to keep them out but rather to give them a future of exploration as they were opened one at a time. She smiled at the thought of Jerry, a perpetual child, keeping their minds filled with wonder while their families abandoned them.

Grace felt a jab of respect for him, he was truly greater than she had given him credit for and she had always held him in the highest regards. She could almost see a shadow of herself beneath all the debris, happy. She smiled into the clutter at her feet, reaching for a shiny rock that she remembered pulling from the pond out back under the willow tree.

A hand pulled at her arm, she looked up into King's dark eyes. "You alright Grace?" He asked snapping her back into the dim reality.

She nodded, pulling herself together blinking at the blue of the hallway as her eyes refocused on the scene before her. She stepped over the debris of the tumbled box and caught up to Ethan, glancing back at King with disappointment.

She could have looked through those things for hours, she hoped she would get the chance to see her treasures again when this was all over. Looking at her hand she smiled at the shiny rock. Tucking it into one of Chung's many coat pockets for later, just in case she didn't get a chance to come back.

Ethan fumbled through the cluttered hallway to the spare room where Grace had stayed on nights when her father was away. It was practically her home away from home. Most of her things had been kept there because of the frequency of her trips to the Evans' estate. He pushed at the door clearing the rubbish that had gathered behind it enough to wedge the door open. The room was filled with boxes and furniture surrounding her four post bed, made up just the way she had left it with her teddy sitting on the pillow in the middle.

Grace wondered for a moment if anyone had even been in there since her disappearance. Judging by the piles of boxes and mismatched furniture smelling of wet charred wood she guessed someone had; by the looks of it only very recently and only for the storage of damaged things from the fire.

Ethan tried to clear a path for her. *He* hadn't been in that room since the day Grace had disappeared. Jerry had eventually taken to using it as storage, giving him an excuse to stay clear as Grace's things had gathered dust in her absence.

Sometimes Ethan would stand at her door, hand on the doorknob fighting with himself to open it. Just to see if she would be there, sitting in her bed like nothing had happened. Sometimes he hoped that it would be true but he never did open the door until today.

Wafting through the air with the stench of the storage and dust were memories of sneaking into Grace's room and sleeping in her bed when there was a thunderstorm. They would pull back the curtains at the window and sleep with their heads at the foot of the bed watching the lightning and giving the shapes names.

Now the curtains were drawn and the windows boarded over. The furniture was lazily draped with old sheets to stave off the impending doom of the thick layer of dust that had all but seeped into every nook and cranny of the room.

HOME

King handed Grace his flashlight as she climbed over the clutter and stacks of boxes into her old room. The years had changed it, yet underneath the piles of boxes and swaths of fabric over the furniture, it was still the room she remembered. It still felt safe to her and she could tell by the dusty white sheets over one of the bed posts that the fire had not damaged her room in the slightest.

She groped over to the pile covering the closet door, struggling as teetering boxes threatened to collapse in on her and plumes of dust wafted up in clouds whenever she brushed past anything too closely.

Ethan was already moving things quickly into another pile. She began picking up boxes and moving them aside, trying to hold her breath against the thickness of the air.

Soon the door was clear enough for them to wedge open, getting inside was another story. Grace flashed her light inside to assess the situation. The closet was filled with dusty clothes and shoes none of them belonging to her. Old work boots and hole-filled dress shoes littered the space in mounds, toppling over into the free space where the door had swung open.

Grace climbed over them passing a couple of larger pairs out through the door for Ethan to discard. She felt along the back wall for the catch that would open the secret compartment. It clicked and the back wall swung away from her.

Shoes collapsed into the new space. Grace shoved them aside, tossing more out of the closet door for Ethan to move. She crawled forward flashing her light at the hardwood in the small cavity passing back several more shoes to make more room as she tried to find the niche.

She tried three floorboards before finding the right one. It was stiffer to pull back than when she had used it ten years ago to hide the files. Squishing her hand into the tiny crevasse she felt the stack, dusty and slippery.

One by one she twisted the files out, placing them in a pile beside her. It was a tedious process because she had to roll each file up with one hand to fit it through the small opening.

"What's going to happen after you get the files?" Ethan asked while Grace dug through the closet.

King scratched his chin, "Take them in. The bureau will start a case against Hart..." He looked at the closet door. The dim light of his flashlight bounced off the wall. "You and Grace will be put into protective custody until the case comes to trial. And after all this, you two are going to be heavily guarded. I think you might need it..." His eyes went wide as he shook his head in disbelief of the events of the previous days.

"She'll be safe though?" Ethan asked concern rising in his voice, too low for Grace to hear over the creaking of the boards and the subtle squeaking of the shoes under her knees.

"You will *both* be safe." King assured, "I'll make sure of it." He promised, with definite intention.

Ethan felt a surge of relief, he truly believed in agent King's word. The man had gone through hell and back to help him rescue Grace and he was willing to bet their safety was going to be a similar adventure over the next several months as things came to terms with Hart's business associates.

Dangerous people were going to be coming out of the woodwork and he and Grace were surely the ones with bulls eyes painted on their heads. The protection of the bureau was imperative. A point he had stressed to agent King even before they had launched their over the wall assault in the first place, King now understood why.

Platt and Peters had called in an entourage to escort them to safety after they left the Evans estate. With all the trials that had pressed them over the last two days, they took extra precaution and insisted on the armoured vehicles.

Grace and Ethan were going straight to a safe house inside the local bureau building where they could ensure their protection and well being on a round the clock basis. They would be assessed from there and moved out accordingly, it was bound to be a long journey ahead of them.

***

Twenty minutes later Grace emerged from the closet with a stack of paper. Her hands were raw with splinters and paper cuts. Her eyes red from the dust clouds she stirred every time she lifted a folder through the cracks. She held the flashlight in her teeth, teetering over the shoes as it pointed at the floor in a blue beam.

Her arms were loaded with the now folded and worn pages tucked into their soft manila folders for what little protection they had provided against the elements. It was a lucky thing her closet had remained untouched by the fire, or the water damage caused by putting it out. Hart had certainly had the right idea trying to burn the house to ashes. These papers were worth more than the house itself, a sprawling mansion put into perspective against a stack of paper.

"The motherload." Whispered King, holding his hand out to help Grace back through the pile and into a clearing in the bedroom.

She spit the flashlight into his hand so he could hold it up for her, giving her a chance to check her footing as she crossed over the teetering boxes and hap hazardously piled chairs, covered in drooping linens. As she fumbled her way through to the door she sighed in relief, looking longingly to her guest bed covered in dust and still waiting for her.

She yearned to crawl up in it and wait for this all to wash over like a storm filled with lightning and thunder. She turned back to the door and continued on, away from the bed.

It had taken her ten years to get these into the right hands and as she passed the pile over to King she felt relief washing over her. *Let someone else worry about these files for a while*, she thought, letting the flimsy pile of papers fall into Kings waiting arms.

He looked at her with wide eyes, peeking into the first file he skimmed past a few lines, mouth dropping. He now held her father's hit list from ten years ago. Ethan's fathers name sat at the top with a red circle around it. Grace assumed many of the names that followed were familiar to King as he muttered under his breath in awe at the first page on the stack.

Normally her father would burn these writings after a meeting, leaving it all in his head with no paper trail was always safer. However extenuating circumstances had left him rushing from his office as Grace hid in a cupboard fearful of being found. When she had approached his desk in horror after having heard the dealings behind his oak doors for the first time, this was the list that had caught her attention.

She had intended to take it straight to Ethan for interpretation, she hadn't known how dangerous those papers would be in her hands or that the consequences of looking at them would be life-long. Her father had gotten to her first.

ESCAPE

Taking Ethan's hand in hers, she smiled and pulled him in for a hug over a mound of sheets. They filtered back out into the hallway clamouring over the pile of discarded refuse Ethan had tossed across the room to free up the closet doorway.

The hallway seemed surprisingly cheerful now that they were about to leave the desolate house, finally in possession of the one thing that Hart couldn't dispute; his own written accounts and a daughter who wouldn't stay buried.

Grace almost walked with a spring in her step as she danced through the scattered junk on the hall and landing. If the banister didn't look about ready to go she would gleefully slide down it for nostalgia's sake.

She vowed that if she made it out of this nightmare she would come back and slide down the railing, after jumping on her old bed one last time.

***

Hart pulled up behind the battered SUV's that were falling to pieces in front of the Evans' estate. As he stepped from the car he pulled his gun out checking the chamber quietly for bullets. He held it at his side tucked up into his suit sleeve.

Hart looked to the decaying house, snarling at the charred window frames and he hoped he had done enough damage. He had known those pages were there but it was awfully hard to burn a house down twice without raising suspicion.

If the fire didn't do the job, perhaps the water from putting out the blaze had helped destroy them enough to make the pages inadmissible as evidence.

The front steps had lost their grandeur to him long before they had started to decay. There had come a day when he was no longer welcome at this place and he could feel it creeping over him as he looked at the gaping door.

With a sharp nod to his accomplice he started up the steps two at a time. The door was ajar and he stepped through as the pounding footsteps of his daughter and her companions reached the bottom of the winding staircase talking amongst themselves with a prideful banter, unaware of his presence.

Hart was taken back for a moment, remembering the same fiery haired little girl prancing gleefully down those very stairs to greet him after long business trips filled with murder and pain. For a brief moment he regretted what he had turned her in to. Looking at her now however, he could see that she was still the same wide eyed girl he had loved before she betrayed him.

"Hello Grace." He drawled stopping in the centre of the grand foyer with his feet resting on a large crack that lined the otherwise breathtaking marble floor. Hart felt like he was standing at the centre of her universe now. They couldn't leave without passing him; it was time that they faced each other at long last.

"Father." Her voice was commanding and dark. She took the final step standing at the base of the stairs before her companions like a cold statue.

"And what brings you to the Evans' estate?" He smirked, tapping his foot impatiently at the required pleasantries. "It appears I should have put a little more effort into burning the place down." He chuckled as Grace boldly approached him.

"It feels nice to be home." Grace watched the disappointment wash quickly over her father's face at the comment.

He had never been home when she was young. She had spent most of her time here with Ethan.

Grace paused five feet from her father. The pale moonlight dimly lit the foyer through the open main doors. The light hit Grace, lighting her up like a ghostly angel standing before her father looking for justice. She stood still with her hands at her side. Damp clothing, ripped and torn, hung from her delicate frame like wings draped over her back. There was a gleam in her eyes that held Hart's gaze for a moment too long. Her presence was intimidating, her willpower horrifying.

"It is over." She declared, standing her ground as her father lifted his hand and pulled the trigger.

FINALE

Grace fell delicately to the ground like a petal in the pale moon light. The bullet had grazed her waist twisting her like a ballerina as she tumbled. She landed facing Ethan at the foot of the stairs with her matted hair draped across the floor catching the moonlight in its tangled locks.

Hart walked to his fallen daughter looking down on her with pleasure.

"It's not over until I say it is." He hissed.

Snapping his fingers over his shoulder, his henchman walked in. He was a burly and intimidating man under any other circumstances. However, he looked scared to be entering the dilapidated home. Even more terrified to see that he was up against the three men at the stairs, and now with the two coming back into the foyer from the kitchen the full gravity of his situation had sunk in. He stood his ground like a good thug waiting for Hart's direction.

Ethan ran to Grace, holding her hand he whispered to her, "Don't give up yet, Grace. I need you. Don't give up, please."

As he brushed her hair from her face, careful not to touch her too harshly. He hadn't seen where the bullet had struck and was terrified that these were his final moments with her, "I love you." He whispered, leaning in so only she could hear him in the chaos.

Ethan closed his eyes for a moment holding his head in to Grace's soft hair. His breath caught as he tried to breathe. Grief washed over him before he looked down to see Grace looking back up into his eyes smiling through the pain with tears in her eyes.

Hart looked down on the two of them, disgusted by the boy's dedication to his snivelling daughter. He looked to the armed men standing at the base of the stairs, too slow to have stopped him and he smiled with satisfaction.

Grace looked into Ethan's deep grey eyes and she knew she wanted to spend forever unraveling the life behind them. She didn't want to miss another minute of time with him and she couldn't give up now.

Grace gripped his hand tight, holding it as she stood with her other hand clutching at her side stifling the flow of blood. She held Ethan close glaring daggers at her father and his henchman. Standing her ground she walked towards him.

He staggered slightly taking a step back, not expecting Grace to have so much fight left in her. Platt had stepped between Grace and her father, holding his gun firmly at her father's head. "Drop the weapon, Sir." He demanded in his most official voice.

King hung in back with the stack of files, hiding them from sight behind the rickety banister while he talked in hurried hushed tones on the phone pressed against his ear. His eyes darted across the room, taking in the whole scene several times as he described every detail of the mess to the technician on the other end of the line.

Ethan wrapped his arm around Grace, holding her up. He knew she was trying to be strong so he let her stand on her own, staying close if she needed him. She looked as though *she* was supporting *him* and he smiled at the thought of having her close to him when this all blew over.

He had missed her and he hadn't known how much until her father had struck her down before him. Ethan wasn't going anywhere and he wasn't about to let Grace out of his sight any time soon.

Six armed men swooped in through the front door surrounding Hart and his man. They grabbed him, wrapping his arms behind his back to cuff him.

Hart locked eyes with Grace as they took him to the door, "It's not over." He hissed, smiling as they dragged him away into the light of the moon.

Grace smiled; *this will be over soon enough*, she thought. Grace stood like an avenging angel, calm and peaceful, while men stirred around her. She watched as her father was taken into custody, waiting until he was out of sight before she stepped back to the staircase and collapsed in a heap onto a step. She clutched at her side, curling into Ethan as she pulled him down with her.

"I love you too." She smiled into his dark eyes. They stared out the front door at the low moon over the scraggly lawn for a moment before more men came rushing through the doors and the whole house was lit up like a circus.

Men swarmed into the building searching, setting up lights and taking statements. Paramedics came rushing in behind them. Grace and Ethan stayed still, looking at each other for the first time in years.

Ethan looked into Grace's damp eyes and whispered, "I've always loved you."

Grace pulled herself up to kiss him.

***

Paramedics had looked Grace over. She was stitched up in the ambulance for good measure. King insisted that Grace and Ethan stayed in a safe house until the case had gone to court.

ESCAPE

He was on the phone making arrangements with his office. He and his partner would be staying close. Chung had woken up and was set to be released in less than a week. King had been on the phone with the hospital when it had happened.

Chung seemed pretty relieved that his hard work had paid off this well. He would have to wait for the rest of the story until he was out. King was afraid of giving him a heart attack, and he was still in pretty bad condition.

King looked over the files before he had to hand them in to his senior officer. Kidnapping, murders, embezzlement: Hart had been involved in a great deal of shady business.

In King's opinion killing off your own daughter and locking her away in a tower topped the list pretty well. Hart was going away for a very long time. And *he* was going for a very long shower when he got home. As the adrenalin and caffeine slowly wore off he could feel his eyes growing heavy.

He took a ride in the back of one of the vans, closing his eyes only once. He woke up at the office sure that he had only blinked. After forty eight hours like he had had, he felt that he could sleep for a week. He probably would, his schedule had already been cleared for him.

He smiled as his co-workers patted him on the back on his way in, all dying to hear of his gallant rescue mission. He felt like James Bond in all the commotion of his return to the office. But they too would have to wait for the story, he needed to go for de-briefing first. Walking past his desk on the way to the back office, he looked down at it one last time, knowing that by tomorrow the corner cubicle would be moving on to a new agent. He patted his wall as he passed, smiling.

***

Grace settled into her secret life under house arrest like a professional. Having spent ten years locked away, the situation seemed a nice transition into her soon to be free life, giving her a chance to adjust to all the new technology and catch up on some of the life that she had missed.

It felt strange knowing that if she were to be tossed back into her old life this very moment she probably wouldn't know what to do with it. She wasn't ten years old anymore; grade school was long gone for her. She had skipped middle school and high school. Most of her old classmates were in college or university. Some of them had even settled into life as adults.

Having Ethan for company greatly improved her demeanor. He was able to help her figure out little things, like how to use a touch phone, or a computer; how to change the channels on the television. She was baffled with how technological every day things had become.

Grace was finally happy, taking time to enjoy the little things she had missed over the years, like bubble baths. She had a lot to catch up on and was looking forward to every step. She spent nights curled up on the couch with Ethan practicing reading children's books while they watched re-runs of Shark Week over and over. *How had she gone this long without knowing all of this?* She thought to herself smiling.

The safe house itself was little more than a bungalow on a dead end street. The fence in the back had been electrified and the furniture, though minimal to others, was extravagant and lush compared to the lumpy bed Grace had used in her tower.

This was considered their high security risk placement. There had been cameras installed all over the outside of the house in almost every tree and bush. Sometimes when Grace was close to a window she would look at them and make faces, thinking King and Chung might be a the other end watching. Whoever was probably thought she was strange but it helped fill the time up for her and Ethan, sneaking through the house without being seen from the outside cameras.

They would crawl past the windows laughing at their bad ninja skills when they were spotted by the agent on duty at the house. He would sit reading his paper with a stoic stare on his serious face until he looked up and caught Ethan or Grace rolling across the floor under the window; coffee would spill down his chin as he laughed, clutching his side.

Grace took pleasure walking from room to room and sitting on every chair, noting the firmness or softness of the fabric and cushion. Whenever Ethan caught her doing this he would start laughing and she would go flush with embarrassment. Still, she enjoyed having more than one place to sit and the luxury of company was not lost on her. She would talk and talk to anyone in the room for hours and she liked listening even more. Hearing the sound of someone else's voice was something she had missed in her imprisonment. Talking out loud to herself had never filled the void of someone else's spoken thoughts.

Grace would stand for hours with the fridge door swung open deciding what she would try next. After ten years of rice and protein shakes she was thrilled to have real food again. The different textures and tastes were euphoric to her bland taste buds. She often found herself taking small tastes of many things until she was full rather than eating a real meal.

Even the water tasted better, cold from the tap and not filled with rust and white clouds like she had become accustomed to. Everything made her smile and at times she found her cheeks sore from all of it. But not even that could stop the grin plastered across her face from staying put.

King and Chung had stayed in touch with them, calling every day to check in on them. Two new agents, Kramer and Wilkinson, had been stationed in the house with them for their safety. The situation was strenuous on the new agents. The case King was working on was very high profile and put Grace and Ethan on several hit lists; there were people who could not afford to let this case be opened let alone brought to trial.

Two times they had packed Grace and Ethan up in the night and moved them to a new location; Hart had business partners who would not *allow* the case to go to trial and they would do just about anything to stop the ball from rolling forward.

Grace had taken to avoiding the windows after she locked eyes with a strange man in their backyard one night. That had been their first move. Since then she had kept all the blinds closed and Ethan close by her side. Their games of window ninja had come to an abrupt stop quickly becoming a more serious avoidance of any place that they could be seen from the outside because of the targets on their backs.

They took to quieter activities to pass the time. Ethan was trying to teach Grace multiplication, it was something she had missed out on when she had been ripped from her old life. She spent hours poring over fake homework assignments Ethan and Wilkinson would make for her trying to solve the problems on her own.

She wanted to get up to par with the children she had grown up away from. She wanted to know what they knew. Sometimes she would become frustrated when a particular question remained unanswered before her for too long.

"If you have three sets of three." Ethan explained one night. "That makes nine. So, three times three would be nine, see?"

Grace scribbled onto her piece of paper making sense of it as she nodded. She looked back up to Ethan with a smile still plastered across her face.

Grace leaned in for a kiss. "Thank you for not treating me like an idiot, I feel so far behind." She brushed her lips against his lightly.

"No problem." He pulled her in so their foreheads touched, "And I felt pretty far behind when you had to save me from the cellar." He smiled "You were always the knight in shining armor Grace." He brushed a strand of hair from her face delicately.

"And *you* were always my princess." She laughed, pulling him in closer again.

SAFE

Soon Grace had more pressing issues to deal with as she was escorted by guards twice a week to meet with her attorney. This case was going to be very public and she was preparing for the long-term consequences. Having been legally dead for the past ten years left a lot of questions to be answered in the eyes of the law; her name, education and inheritance had all fallen wayside when she had been presumed dead.

Given the gravity of her father's actions the trial would likely leave her with enough to get by for the rest of her life but Grace wanted more. She wanted the education she had missed out on. She wanted to keep her identity and she wanted more than anything to move on. Grace wanted to save other people, but first she had to finish saving herself.

Luckily with the help of some of Hart's men that had been taken alive they had pinpointed locations of some of his other facilities and three other missing people had been found alive. All of which had been set to stand trial against one criminal or another before their disappearances. Most of the cases had been dropped when the key witnesses had gone missing.

It was an ingenious business plan for Hart: if you could pay someone to hide your opposition for long enough, the case wouldn't hold up in court. Grace even considered her father's methods more humane than the alternative. Although purely evil, at least he kept most of his victims alive until their court dates blew over. Then he would ship them off to Mexico or Europe in cargo and have them unexpectedly show up back on the radar looking like they had bailed on the courts of their own free will. Still, the cases had all been closed and he and his business companions would continue swindling money out of others pockets for another day.

This case was getting bigger every day as more names from the list were found and investigated; the cases were all linking together. Nearly all of the crimes filed away ten years ago were accounted for on Grace's pages.

Mr. Hart had been running a shady business of kidnapping those in opposition to his business morals by faking their deaths or as in Mr Evans' case, killing them. As the names and dates began to line up Grace's attorney became more flustered, arriving with her own entourage of security one day.

It was then that Grace began to realize the dangers she was in standing against these men. Her team of one slowly became a team of five, and then ten as the list of criminals became longer and longer. They were fighting for more victims than just Grace. She soon met some of the other survivors, mostly conversing through Skype and other online correspondence. Even she was not permitted to leave the safe house for these meetings. She was under house arrest until the court date finally arrived.

Months passed, seasons changes, and Grace waited until the day arrived when she was finally called upon to put her father's actions to justice.

She relished the moments of fresh air as she walked to the armoured van, arriving at the court through a back entrance. She was kept in a locked room with the other witnesses surrounded by guards until the case required her.

Each day that Grace appeared in court Ethan was there to support her. Sitting between King and Chung for security, he was not allowed out of the house without a guard any more than she was. And each day that her eyes locked with her father's she felt pity for him.

He was going to find out just how difficult it was being locked away in a tower but he was going to have very unhappy company with him. With his conviction he had taken with him a ring of crime bosses and several companies involved in staffing his kidnapping business.

Reporters wanted to hear from Grace, swarming at her each day as she left the courthouse through the back entrance. She held her chin high and her lips pressed tight as she passed them by.

She wanted her story to be told but she wanted it told on her terms, sparing no details. She would bide her time until it was the right moment to share her suffering with the world, when her situation might help someone else who was suffering. Not for publicity or fame, she was not going to be portrayed as a victim.

Grace was going to be the survivor.

***

The trial passed with little effort from their side. They were a clear winner from the jump off. Three years of lawyers and courtrooms were still heaven compared to three years locked in her father's prison. The day the case was finally closed Grace felt a rush of relief. She watched with quiet pride as her father was escorted out of the room in his formal jumpsuit for the last time. She held Ethan's hand tightly under the table, he smiled to her whispering, "See? You did it."

She nodded.

As they exited the courtroom that day agent King turned and took Grace's hand in his. Looking at the proud smiling young woman before him he felt pride in his accomplishments. She had been stronger than he had given her credit for. He still remembered the scraggly young girl that had been running toward her freedom only three years ago. Now standing before him in a clean cut suit with her wispy locks of twisted orange tucked behind her ear, it was hard to imagine they were one and the same. He looked at her with pride in his tired eyes.

"Congratulations Grace." He smiled with a crinkling at the eyes, "It's finally over"

Her wild grin was contagious. She was finally starting a life that had been paused at ten. As she tugged King in for a bear hug holding him tight a tear trickled down her cheek across her gaping grin. She was so lucky to have met someone as dedicated as King was. He had pulled every string in his power to keep her and Ethan together while they fought tooth and nail for their freedom.

She wasn't sure she would ever be able to repay him for the help he had provided for her in her darkest hours. She looked to him like the father she wished she had had and felt ashamed that she had nothing to offer him in return. At the very least he had gotten the promotion he had been wanting for all those years. She was glad to have helped him achieve it. She had sent in written recommendations and letters of praise from her safe house to help push the process along for him and Chung; anything for the two men that had literally taken bullets for her.

"Thank you for everything." She reached for an embarrassed Chung pulling him in close, "Both of you." She was still tearing up with joy as the two grown men were pressed together by her scrawny arms. "This means everything." She continued as her teary eyes looked to King's, catching him off guard with their wide eyed wonder.

He looked away quickly, willing himself not to tear up in her presence; Chung would never let him live it down if he started crying.

Chung backed out of the embrace, patting Grace delicately on the shoulder. He smiled sincerely reaching to an inside pocket of his signature black suit. He pulled forth a card taking Grace's hand he placed the card in her palm folding her fingers over the piece of ridged cardstock as he lowered his eyes.

"You remember to keep in touch now." He smiled at her letting her hand go. She looked down at the new business numbers on the card, smiling at the Washington address. They had finally moved up the ladder.

Over the months Ethan and Grace had grown close to King and Chung. Asides from their daily check in phone call they often found themselves meeting up once or twice a week within the safety of their house to watch movies or catch the latest wrestling match.

Chung had even taken to coming by a few times a week on his own to teach Grace the basics of boxing, his own favourite past time. She was starting to pick it up quickly. Demonstrating a dedication that Chung admitted most students were lacking. She had already fought for her life and lost and now she had the determination to never lose again.

That desire had powered her through several embarrassing pin downs where she had rendered Chung useless. It was a good thing she had a kind heart because power like hers in any other hands could be dangerous indeed.

Although the agents were moving on to a new city with their promotion, Grace knew she would continue to keep in touch with the unlikely companions who had helped her get her life back from the disastrous brink of death.

Ethan hovered behind Grace and with a stern nod he reached out to shake King's hand and awkwardly settled for a fist bump from Chung. He seemed to be in a state of shock as it hadn't quite occurred to him that the trial was over and life with Grace was about to resume after a long pause of nearly thirteen years.

He had a look about him like he was frozen with butterflies in his stomach or terrified of something in the imminent future looming closer by the second as they were soon to exit the courthouse forever. He fidgeted with his keys in the pocket of his suit jacket. The heat had him sweating as he waited patiently to take the jacket off and cool down a bit.

"Later." Chung turned, walking down the long hallway with a wave back over his shoulder.

King trailed after him pausing to remind Ethan with a smirk. "See you soon."

Grace laughed as he continued out the doors walking quickly to catch up to Chung who was likely his ride out of there. Grace watched as their heads bobbed away down the steps and out of sight.

Ethan took Grace by the hand; "I have something to show you." He smiled as they walked to his car. It had been recently fixed with new windows but it still looked like a pile of junk. Sitting in the parking lot it looked like a piece of evidence in a gruesome car accident, scraps of metal pieced together like a robotic Frankenstein's monster. It was a creation that looked as though it were impersonating a piece of tacky lawn art.

He opened the passenger door for Grace with an elegant wave of his hand bowing at the waist and grinning ear to ear. Stepping back he reached into the back seat to pull out a slightly wilted bouquet of pink and yellow roses. The leaves had wilted and the baby's breath that accompanied it was squished into an awkward salute.

"For you." He kissed her as he placed the roses in her hands. Ethan walked to the driver side and after a couple of embarrassing attempts he started the car, sending a billowing cloud of smoke out the back exhaust.

Grace smiled at the flowers. She was still emotional from the day's events and her father's incarceration. As she brought the bouquet to her face and took in a deep breath she began to feel calmer. The smell of flowers had long eluded her during her years of confinement, but Ethan had been bribing the guards to bring her bouquets for almost a year now.

Being hidden in the safe house she hadn't had the chance to re-unite with the garden scents of her past and here she finally held her first bouquet of freedom in her arms. The scent was strong and warm in the heated air. It was arguably the best thing she had ever smelt.

Ethan's car had been towed from the side of the forest three years earlier with no windows and most of the parts stripped from the engine. Local scavengers had picked through all of the components leaving him with only the rusty husk of his father's old car. With the help of King, while Grace practiced boxing, he had slowly pieced it back together in the garage of the safe house. Thanks to King, who had sent in a special request to have it towed from impound and transferred with them through the multiple locations they had occupied.

Ethan still had work to do but this car had been his fathers and had driven Grace and Ethan around town in their early years. The sentimental value greatly outweighed the cost and time to repair it. He could remember a time when they had gone to a drive-in movie, spilling popcorn all over the floor. When Jerry had given him the keys at sixteen he had found un-popped kernels under the driver seat and smiled at the memory.

Grace was familiar with the roads winding through the town. The trees had changed over the years but the bulk had remained the same. Sunlight shone through branches that blocked a perfect blue sky. Grace rolled her window down letting a gentle summer breeze rustle her hair and cool her warm cheeks. Life was ready to begin anew; she could feel great things in her future, now that she had one. She smiled into the wind.

Ethan pulled up in front of the Evans Estate. Grace hadn't seen the house since the night her father had shot her, still bearing the scar on her waist. The exterior looked as if it was being renovated. Scaffolding lined the outer walls in patches and the house looked calm and bright in the warm mid day.

Light reflected off of the new windows bright and cheery compared to the dull luster of the boards that had once lined them. The dark smoke rings had all been washed away and the mortar refreshed and repaired. The grounds were once again neatly kept with flowers blooming in the August heat. A trail of pink petals lay in sweet disarray on the front steps that were looking fresh and grand once again.

Grace looked on in shock at the changes of the mansion and how different it looked in new light after the horror of that night. Ethan had swooped around the car and opened her door to take her hand before she even noticed they had stopped moving.

Kneeling before her at the foot of the decorated stairs he took a small box from his back pocket.

"Grace Hart, I have known you all my life and missed you more than anything for almost half of it. You once called this your home." He looked back to the mansion, remembering her defiant words to her father in the moon lit foyer, "I cannot imagine having to live another day without you by my side." He paused for a moment, catching his breath as it caught in his throat, "Grace, would you do me the honor of calling this *our* house, will you marry me?"

Ethan opened the pale grey box. Inside was his mothers engagement ring; a large princess diamond cut with two pink stones on either side. It looked like a fairy ring and reminded Grace of all the love Ethan's family had extended to her over the years. Tears welled up in her bright green eyes.

"Yes." She whispered throwing herself forward into Ethan's arms.

Ethan slipped the ring onto her tiny finger. It would have to be resized for her pixie like hand. He lifted her into his arms as they both looked up to the grand mansion before them. He carried her up the front steps of their home. Slowly and carefully he held her close to his chest as they walked through the large front doors into the well lit foyer. The chandelier gleamed back at them as Ethan gently placed Grace back on her feet.

Jerry stood in the foyer standing properly beside a well-worn golf bag.

"You're late for our tea party miss." He joked.

Jumping from Ethan's arms Grace ran to Jerry nearly knocking him down with her excitement.

"Jerry, I'm so glad to see you." She mused, "Please tell us you can stay for a while." She begged of him.

He looked nearly the same as she remembered him. He had aged well, still looking as young as he had been when he snuck out marshmallows to their campfires on summer nights long ago. Holding him close she looked him over carefully making sure he was really there.

She had spoken to him on the phone a couple of times since her daring rescue from the tower but this was the first she had seen him in over thirteen years. He looked just as thrilled to see her, holding her hands as they stood at arm's length looking one another over for what must have been an awkward couple of minutes.

Ethan cleared his throat raising an eyebrow as they looked his way suddenly snapping out of their daze and back into focus in the real world.

"I'm already settled in miss." He grinned, looking back at Grace sheepishly for having been caught staring. He turned to Ethan proudly like a father. Walking back into the kitchen with Grace and Ethan in tow, he had a pot of fresh tea waiting as always his timing was impeccable. Beside it sat a tray of cookies, all of their favourites from childhood.

Grace couldn't help but be reminded of the times when she would come here for a long stay and how it would always begin like this, sitting in the kitchen having tea and cookies. She smiled, hoping it would be a very long stay indeed.

***

Over the next year the house was fully remodelled to suit Grace and Ethan. Jerry had already had most of the work done before they moved in taking care of the more fundamental renovations, like repairing the water damage from the fire. He worked with Ethan on the telephone to make arrangements and decisions while the court trial had still been raging to ensure the house would be liveable before they were released and ready to move in.

The main floor damage was done making it looked almost the same as Grace remembered from her childhood. The pictures in the hall had been reprinted and framed to look nearly identical while the holes in the staircase had been fixed.

Of course Grace remembered precisely which steps Ethan had fallen through, smiling at his sacrifice for her own sure footing after their disastrous adventure.

Ethan moved his few belongings into Grace's room which had been freshly dusted and fluffed to prepare for her arrival. The clutter had been moved out and it looked as she had left it, only better.

For nostalgias sake they left the master bedroom door closed and locked just as Mr. Evans had always had it, leaving them curious as to what secrets were within.

Ethan had taken extra precautions before their official move-in. He hired a team of security officers from a company King had recommended to monitor the grounds night and day, reporting anything suspicious to Ethan and the local police, who were keen on keeping an eye on the place anyway.

They continued to keep in touch with King and Chung, inviting them over for a few weeks during the unseasonably warm autumn. They had lounged in the sun room where Grace was attempting to start a garden of pink and yellow roses with little luck. Laughing at her futile attempts at gardening while she proved again and again how accident prone she was with gardening equipment, managing to give herself a black eye while repotting a dead rosebush more than once.

***

They held their wedding quietly while King and Chung were visiting. Jerry walked Grace down the petal strewn path, standing in for an absent father who wouldn't have been welcomed even if he wasn't currently behind bars.

Chung and King were the best men bravely holding bouquets of yellow roses by Ethan's side. They held the ceremony in the front yard, under the elegant weeping willow tree where they had liked to play Rapunzel when they were young.

That day however, Grace was finally the princess. The soft white gown she had chosen puffed out at her waist falling like the petals of a white lily to her bare feet. Her hair hung in loose fiery curls down her back as she walked through the veil of willow branches to Ethan with tears in her wondering green eyes. She truly felt as though she had a family for the first time in her life.

For their honeymoon, Ethan and Grace built a fort of twigs and sticks in the backyard where they had played King's Castle as kids. Still wearing her wedding dress and with Ethan in his tux, they brought out blankets and pillows to spend the night watching the stars from the skylights in their magical private honeymoon suite.

"Do you think the stars ever get bored, looking down on everything?" Grace asked Ethan as he wrapped her in his coat.

"Not if they could see you." He whispered, pulling her in. They spent the rest of the night in each other's arms under the stars and the trees.

***

ESCAPE

Two nights after their wedding, when King and Chung had gone back to Washington and Jerry was off to a golf tournament for the week, the front bell rang.

Ethan hadn't heard the noise of the bell in years he hadn't even thought to consider it in the repairs of the house. It sounded warped and sadistic echoing through the halls in an eerie fashion that chilled him to the bone.

He crept from his room where Grace was sleeping soundly under the covers of her four post bed. He was gently padding down the hall when the chime came again, whoever it was sounded impatient. Ethan hurried, afraid of waking Grace if the chime sounded again.

Swinging the front door open he looked into the dusky sky across the vacant front yard. No one stood on the front stoop. Peering cautiously out the door he saw a dark figure walking away into the night down the long driveway cloaked from sight under a heavy trench coat. About to close the door, he looked down.

A square box lay neatly on the outside mat, with a card tucked precisely into the twine that tied it. The card read *"Ethan"* in a delicate scroll that he had seen before. He stooped to pick it up with a last glance out the door as he closed it to the meek night.

Ethan quietly padded to the kitchen taking a perch on one of the stools at the counter. He placed the curious package in front of him and stared at it for a moment longer before reaching for the card. The paper was old and worn, as if it had been written years ago and placed in storage.

Opening it he found that the paper within was not old at all, instead it was crisp and white with fancy scalloped edges. He turned it over once noticing the same delicate scroll, handwritten in expensive ink.

You may have saved the Princess but you have forgotten the King, dear Prince.

Ethan felt a chill roll up his spine as the paper fell to the floor.

ABOUT THE AUTHOR

Katlin Murray lives in Cambridge Ontario with her family, she enjoys reading to her children and watching old movies with her husband.